About the Author

Born and raised in England, CLIVE BARKER, is the internationally bestselling author of twenty books, ranging in subject from epic adult horror fiction to the award-winning modern classic children's series Abarat. Also a widely acclaimed artist and film producer, he is best known as the writer and director of the 1987 cult classic horror film *Hellraiser*, a film which explores the themes of sadomasochism, pain as a source of pleasure, and morality under duress and fear. The film is based on Barker's critically acclaimed novella *The Hellbound Heart* and is the first in the Hellraiser series, having spawned seven sequels as of 2006, with a remake of the original announced in 2007. The movie was ranked number nineteen on Bravo's list of the "100 Scariest Movie Moments." Clive makes his home in Beverly Hills, California.

Visit him on his Web site at www.clivebarker.info.

BOOKS BY CLIVE BARKER

Galilee

Forms of Heaven

Sacrament

Incarnations

Everville

The Thief of Always

Imajica

The Great and Secret Show

The Hellbound Heart

The Books of Blood, Volumes I-III

In the Flesh

The Inhuman Condition

The Damnation Game

Weaveworld

Cabal

Coldheart Canyon

Abarat

Abarat: Days of Magic, Nights of War

CLIVE BARKER

THE HELLBOUND HEART

HARPER

NEW YORK • LONDON • TORONTO • SYDNEY

HARPER

A previous edition of this book was published in 1991 by HarperPaperbacks, an imprint of HarperCollins Publishers.

THE HELLBOUND HEART. Copyright © 1986 by Clive Barker. All rights reserved. Printed in the United States of America. No part of this book may be used or reproduced in any manner whatsoever without written permission except in the case of brief quotations embodied in critical articles and reviews. For information, address HarperCollins Publishers, 195 Broadway, New York, NY 10007.

HarperCollins books may be purchased for educational, business, or sales promotional use. For information, please e-mail the Special Markets Department at SPsales@harpercollins.com.

REISSUED IN HARPER PAPERBACK 2007.

Library of Congress Cataloging-in-Publication Data is available upon request.

ISBN: 978-0-06-145288-8 (reissue)
ISBN-10: 0-06-145288-2 (reissue)

23 24 25 26 27 LBC 38 37 36 35 34

for Mary

I long to talk with some old lover's ghost
Who died before the god of Love was born.

—John Donne, *Love's Deitie*

THE HELLBOUND HEART

ONE

So intent was Frank upon solving the puzzle of Lemarchand's box that he didn't hear the great bell begin to ring. The device had been constructed by a master craftsman, and the riddle was this—that though he'd been told the box contained wonders, there simply seemed to be no way into it, no clue on any of its six black lacquered faces as to the whereabouts of the pressure points that would disengage one piece of this three-dimensional jigsaw from another.

Frank had seen similar puzzles—mostly in Hong Kong, products of the Chinese taste for making metaphysics of hard wood—but to the acuity and technical genius of the Chinese the Frenchman had brought a perverse logic that was entirely his own. If there was a system to the puzzle, Frank had failed to find it. Only after several hours of trial and error did a chance juxtaposition of thumbs, middle and last fingers bear fruit: an almost imperceptible click, and then—victory!—a segment of the box slid out from beside its neighbors.

There were two revelations.

The first, that the interior surfaces were brilliantly polished. Frank's reflection—distorted, fragmented—skated across the lacquer. The second, that Lemarchand, who had been in his time a maker of singing birds, had constructed the box so that opening it tripped a musical mechanism, which began to tinkle a short rondo of sublime banality.

Encouraged by his success, Frank proceeded to work on the box feverishly, quickly finding fresh alignments of fluted slot and oiled peg which in their turn revealed further intricacies. And with each solution—each new half twist or pull—a further melodic element was brought into play—the tune counterpointed and developed until the initial caprice was all but lost in ornamentation.

At some point in his labors, the bell had begun to ring—a steady somber tolling. He had not heard, at least not consciously. But when the puzzle was almost finished—the mirrored innards of the box unknotted—he became aware that his stomach churned so violently at the sound of the bell it might have been ringing half a lifetime.

He looked up from his work. For a few moments he supposed the noise to be coming from somewhere in the street outside—but he rapidly dismissed that notion. It had been almost midnight before he'd begun to work at the birdmaker's box; several hours had gone by—hours he would not have remembered passing but for the evidence of his watch—since then. There was no church in the city—however desperate for adherents—that would ring a summoning bell at such an hour.

No. The sound was coming from somewhere much more distant, through the very door (as yet invisible) that Lemarchand's miraculous box had been constructed to open. Everything that Kircher, who had sold him the box, had promised of it was true! He was on the threshold of a new world, a province infinitely far from the room in which he sat.

Infinitely far; yet now, suddenly near.

The thought had made his breath quick. He had anticipated this moment so keenly, planned with every wit he possessed this rending of the veil. In moments they would be here—the ones Kircher had called the Cenobites, theologians of the Order of the Gash. Summoned from their experiments in the higher reaches of pleasure, to bring their ageless heads into a world of rain and failure.

He had worked ceaselessly in the preceding week to prepare the room for them. The bare boards had been meticulously scrubbed and strewn with petals. Upon the west wall he had set up a kind of altar to them, decorated with the kind of placatory offerings Kircher had assured him would nurture their good offices: bones, bonbons, needles. A jug of his urine— the product of seven days' collection—stood on the left of the altar, should they require some spontaneous gesture of self-defilement. On the right, a plate of doves' heads, which Kircher had also advised him to have on hand.

He had left no part of the invocation ritual unobserved. No cardinal, eager for the fisherman's shoes, could have been more diligent.

But now, as the sound of the bell became louder, drowning out the music box, he was afraid.

Too late, he murmured to himself, hoping to quell his rising fear. Lemarchand's device was undone; the final trick had been turned. There was no time left for prevarication or regret. Besides, hadn't he risked both life and sanity to make this unveiling possible? The doorway was even now opening to pleasures no more than a handful of humans had ever known existed, much less *tasted*—pleasures which would redefine the parameters of sensation, which would release him from the dull round of desire, seduction and disappointment that had dogged him from late adolescence. He would be transformed by that knowledge, wouldn't he? No man could experience the profundity of such feeling and remain unchanged.

The bare bulb in the middle of the room dimmed and brightened, brightened and dimmed again. It had taken on the rhythm of the bell, burning its hottest on each chime. In the troughs between the chimes the darkness in the room became utter; it was as if the world he had occupied for twenty-nine years had ceased to exist. Then the bell would sound again, and the bulb burn so strongly it might never have faltered, and for a few precious seconds he was standing in a familiar place, with a door that led out and down and into the street, and a window through which—had he but the will (or strength) to tear the blinds back—he might glimpse a rumor of morning.

With each peal the bulb's light was becoming more revelatory. By it, he saw the east wall flayed; saw the brick momentarily lose solidity and blow away; saw, in that same instant, the place beyond the room from which the bell's din was issuing. A world of birds was it? Vast black birds caught in perpetual tempest? That was all the sense he could make of the province from which—even now—the hierophants were coming—that it was in confusion, and full of brittle, broken things that rose and fell and filled the dark air with their fright.

And then the wall was solid again, and the bell fell silent. The bulb flickered out. This time it went without a hope of rekindling.

He stood in the darkness, and said nothing. Even if he could remember the words of welcome he'd prepared, his tongue would not have spoken them. It was playing dead in his mouth.

And then, light.

It came from *them:* from the quartet of Cenobites who now, with the wall sealed behind them, occupied the room. A fitful phosphorescence, like the glow of deep-sea fishes: blue, cold, charmless. It struck Frank that he had never once wondered what they would look like. His imagination, though fertile when it came to trickery and theft, was impoverished in other regards. The skill to picture these eminences was beyond him, so he had not even tried.

Why then was he so distressed to set eyes upon them? Was it the scars that covered every inch of their bodies, the flesh cosmetically punctured and sliced and infibulated, then dusted down with ash? Was it the smell of vanilla they brought with them, the sweetness of which did little to disguise the stench beneath? Or was it that as the light grew, and he scanned them more closely, he saw nothing of joy, or even humanity, in their maimed faces: only desperation, and an appetite that made his bowels ache to be voided.

"What city is this?" one of the four enquired. Frank had difficulty guessing the speaker's gender with any certainty. Its clothes, some of which were sewn *to* and *through* its skin, hid its private parts, and there was nothing in the dregs of its voice, or in its willfully disfigured features that offered the least clue. When it spoke, the hooks that transfixed the flaps of its eyes and were wed, by an intricate system of chains passed through flesh and bone alike, to similar hooks through the lower lip, were teased by the motion, exposing the glistening meat beneath.

"I asked you a question," it said. Frank made no reply. The name of this city was the last thing on his mind.

"Do you understand?" the figure beside the first speaker demanded. Its voice, unlike that of its companion, was light and breathy— the voice of an excited girl. Every inch of its head had been tattooed with an intricate grid, and at every intersection of horizontal and vertical axes a jeweled pin driven through to the bone. Its tongue was similarly decorated. "Do you even know who we are?" it asked.

"Yes." Frank said at last. "I know."

Of course he knew; he and Kircher had spent long nights talking of hints gleaned from the diaries of Bolingbroke and Gilles de Rais.

All that mankind knew of the Order of the Gash, he knew.

And yet . . . he had expected something different. Expected some sign of the numberless splendors they had access to. He had thought they would come with women, at least; oiled women, milked women; women shaved and muscled for the act of love: their lips perfumed, their thighs trembling to spread, their buttocks weighty, the way he liked them. He had expected sighs, and languid bodies spread on the floor underfoot like a living carpet; had expected virgin whores whose every crevice was his for the asking and whose skills would press him—*upward, upward*—to undreamed-of ecstasies. The world would be forgotten in their arms. He would be exalted by his lust, instead of despised for it.

But no. No women, no sighs. Only these sexless *things*, with their corrugated flesh.

Now the third spoke. Its features were so heavily scarified—the wounds nurtured until they ballooned—that its eyes were invisible and its words corrupted by the disfigurement of its mouth.

"What do you want?" it asked him.

He perused this questioner more confidently than he had the other two. His fear was draining away with every second that passed. Memories of the terrifying place beyond the wall were already receding. He was left with these decrepit decadents, with their stench, their queer deformity, their self-evident frailty. The only thing he had to fear was nausea.

"Kircher told me there would be five of you," Frank said.

"The Engineer will arrive should the moment merit," came the reply. "Now again, we ask you: *What do you want?*"

Why should he not answer them straight? "Pleasure," he replied. "Kircher said you know about pleasure."

"Oh we do," said the first of them. "Everything you ever wanted."

"Yes?"

"Of course. Of course." It stared at him with its all-too-naked eyes. "What have you dreamed?" it said.

The question, put so baldly, confounded him. How could he hope to articulate the nature of the phantasms his libido had created? He was still searching for words when one of them said:

"This world . . . it disappoints you?"

"Pretty much," he replied.

"You're not the first to tire of its trivialities," came the response. "There have been others."

"Not many," the gridded face put in.

"True. A handful at best. But a few have dared to use Lemarchand's Configuration. Men like yourself, hungry for new possibilities, who've heard that we have skills unknown in your region."

"I'd expected—" Frank began.

"We *know* what you expected," the Cenobite replied. "We understand to its breadth and depth the nature of your frenzy. It is utterly familiar to us."

Frank grunted. "So," he said, "you know what I've dreamed about. You can supply the pleasure."

The thing's face broke open, its lips curling back: a baboon's smile. "Not as you understand it," came the reply.

Frank made to interrupt, but the creature raised a silencing hand.

"There are conditions of the nerve endings," it said, "the like of which your imagination, however fevered, could not hope to evoke."

". . . yes?"

"Oh yes. Oh most certainly. Your most

treasured depravity is child's play beside the experiences we offer."

"Will you partake of them?" said the second Cenobite.

Frank looked at the scars and the hooks. Again, his tongue was deficient.

"Will you?"

Outside, somewhere near, the world would soon be waking. He had watched it wake from the window of this very room, day after day, stirring itself to another round of fruitless pursuits, and he'd known, *known*, that there was nothing left out there to excite him. No heat, only sweat. No passion, only sudden lust, and just as sudden indifference. He had turned his back on such dissatisfaction. If in doing so he had to interpret the signs these creatures brought him, then that was the price of ambition. He was ready to pay it.

"Show me," he said.

"There's no going back. You do understand that?"

"Show me."

They needed no further invitation to raise the curtain. He heard the door creak as it was opened, and turned to see that the world beyond the threshold had disappeared, to be replaced by the same panic-filled darkness from which the members of the Order had stepped. He looked back towards the Cenobites, seeking some explanation for this. But they'd disappeared. Their passing had not gone unrecorded however. They'd taken the flowers with them, leaving only bare boards, and on the wall the offerings he had assembled were blackening, as if in the heat of some fierce but invisible flame. He smelled the bitterness of their consumption; it pricked his nostrils so acutely he was certain they would bleed.

But the smell of burning was only the beginning. No sooner had he registered it than half a dozen other scents filled his head. Perfumes he had scarcely noticed until now were suddenly overpoweringly strong. The lingering scent of filched blossoms; the smell of the paint on the ceiling and the sap in the wood beneath his feet—all filled his head. He could even smell the darkness outside the door, and in it, the ordure of a hundred thousand birds.

He put his hand to his mouth and nose, to stop the onslaught from overcoming him, but the stench of perspiration on his fingers made him giddy. He might have been driven to nausea had there not been fresh sensations flooding his system from each nerve ending and taste bud.

It seemed he could suddenly feel the collision of the dust motes with his skin. Every drawn breath chafed his lips; every blink, his eyes. Bile burned in the back of his throat, and a morsel of yesterday's beef that had lodged between his teeth sent spasms through his system as it exuded a droplet of gravy upon his tongue.

His ears were no less sensitive. His head was filled with a thousand dins, some of which he himself was father to. The air that broke against his eardrums was a hurricane; the flatulence in his bowels was thunder. But there were other sounds—innumerable sounds—which assailed him from somewhere beyond himself. Voices raised in anger, whispered professions of love, roars and rattlings, snatches of song, tears.

Was it the world he was hearing—morning breaking in a thousand homes? He had no chance to listen closely; the cacophony drove any power of analysis from his head.

But there was worse. The eyes! Oh god in heaven, he had never guessed that they could be such torment; he, who'd thought there was nothing on earth left to startle him. Now he reeled! Everywhere, *sight!*

The plain plaster of the ceiling was an

awesome geography of brush strokes. The weave of his plain shirt an unbearable elaboration of threads. In the corner he saw a mite move on a dead dove's head, and wink its eyes at him, seeing that he saw. Too much! *Too much!*

Appalled, he shut his eyes. But there was more *inside* than out; memories whose violence shook him to the verge of senselessness. He sucked his mother's milk, and choked; felt his sibling's arms around him (a fight, was it, or a brotherly embrace? Either way, it suffocated). And more; so much more. A short lifetime of sensations, all writ in a perfect hand upon his cortex, and breaking him with their insistence that they be remembered.

He felt close to exploding. Surely the world outside his head—the room, and the birds beyond the door—they, for all their shrieking excesses, could not be as overwhelming as his memories. Better that, he thought, and tried to open his eyes. But they wouldn't unglue. Tears or pus or needle and thread had sealed them up.

He thought of the faces of the Cenobites: the hooks, the chains. Had they worked some similar surgery upon him, locking him up behind his eyes with the parade of his history?

In fear for his sanity, he began to address them, though he was no longer certain that they were even within earshot.

"*Why?*" he asked. "Why are you doing this to me?"

The echo of his words roared in his ears, but he scarcely attended to it. More sense impressions were swimming up from the past to torment him. Childhood still lingered on his tongue (milk and frustration) but there were adult feelings joining it now. He was grown! He was mustached and mighty, hands heavy, gut large.

Youthful pleasures had possessed the appeal of newness, but as the years had crept on, and mild sensation lost its potency, stronger and stronger experiences had been called for. And here they came again, more pungent for being laid in the darkness at the back of his head.

He felt untold tastes upon his tongue: bitter, sweet, sour, salty; smelled spice and shit and his mother's hair; saw cities and skies; saw speed, saw deeps; broke bread with men now dead and was scalded by the heat of their spittle on his cheek.

And of course there were women.

Always, amid the flurry and confusion,

memories of women appeared, assaulting him
with their scents, their textures, their tastes.

The proximity of this harem aroused him,
despite circumstances. He opened his trousers
and caressed his cock, more eager to have the
seed spilled and so be freed of these creatures
than for the pleasure of it.

He was dimly aware, as he worked his
inches, that he must make a pitiful sight: a
blind man in an empty room, aroused for a
dream's sake. But the wracking, joyless orgasm
failed to even slow the relentless display. His
knees buckled, and his body collapsed to the
boards where his spunk had fallen. There was
a spasm of pain as he hit the floor, but the
response was washed away before another wave
of memories.

He rolled onto his back, and screamed;
screamed and begged for an end to it, but the
sensations only rose higher still, whipped to
fresh heights with every prayer for cessation he
offered up.

The pleas became a single sound, words
and sense eclipsed by panic. It seemed there
was no end to this, but madness. No hope but
to be lost to hope.

As he formulated this last, despairing
thought, the torment stopped.

All at once; all of it. Gone. Sight, sound, touch, taste, smell. He was abruptly bereft of them all. There were seconds then, when he doubted his very existence. Two heartbeats, three, four.

On the fifth beat, he opened his eyes. The room was empty, the doves and the piss-pot gone. The door was closed.

Gingerly, he sat up. His limbs were tingling; his head, wrist, and bladder ached.

And then—a movement at the other end of the room drew his attention.

Where, two moments before, there had been an empty space, there was now a figure. It was the fourth Cenobite, the one that had never spoken, nor shown its face. Not *it*, he now saw: but *she*. The hood it had worn had been discarded, as had the robes. The woman beneath was gray yet gleaming, her lips bloody, her legs parted so that the elaborate scarification of her pubis was displayed. She sat on a pile of rotting human heads, and smiled in welcome.

The collision of sensuality and death appalled him. Could he have any doubt that she had personally dispatched these victims? Their rot was beneath her nails, and their tongues—twenty or more—lay out in ranks on her oiled thighs, as if awaiting entrance. Nor did he doubt that the brains now seeping from their ears and nostrils had been driven to insanity before a blow or a kiss had stopped their hearts.

Kircher had lied to him—either that or he'd been horribly deceived. There was no pleasure in the air; or at least not as humankind understood it.

He had made a mistake opening Lemarchand's box. A very terrible mistake.

"Oh, so you've finished dreaming," said the Cenobite, perusing him as he lay panting on the bare boards. "Good."

She stood up. The tongues fell to the floor, like a rain of slugs.

"Now we can begin," she said.

TWO

"*It's* not quite what I expected," Julia commented as they stood in the hallway. It was twilight; a cold day in August. Not the ideal time to view a house that had been left empty for so long.

"It needs work," Rory said. "That's all. It's not been touched since my grandmother died. That's the best part of three years. And I'm pretty sure she never did anything to it towards the end of her life."

"And it's yours?"

"Mine and Frank's. It was willed to us both. But when was the last time anybody saw big brother?"

She shrugged, as if she couldn't remember, though she remembered very well. A week before the wedding.

"Someone said he spent a few days here last summer. Rutting away, no doubt. Then he was off again. He's got no interest in property."

"But suppose we move in, and then he comes back, wants what's his?"

"I'll buy him out. I'll get a loan from the bank and buy him out. He's always hard up for cash."

She nodded, but looked less than persuaded.

"Don't worry," he said, going to where she was standing and wrapping his arms around her. "The place is ours, doll. We can paint it and pamper it and make it like heaven."

He scanned her face. Sometimes—particularly when doubt moved her, as it did now— her beauty came close to frightening him.

"Trust me," he said.

"I do."

"All right then. What say we start moving in on Sunday?"

Sunday.

It was still the Lord's Day up this end of the city. Even if the owners of these well-dressed houses and well-pressed children were no longer believers, they still observed the sabbath. A few curtains were twitched aside when Lewton's van drew up, and the unloading began; some curious neighbors even sauntered past the house once or twice, on the pretext of walking the hounds; but nobody spoke to the new arrivals, much less offered a hand with the furniture. Sunday was not a day to break sweat.

Julia looked after the unpacking, while Rory organized the unloading of the van, with Lewton and Mad Bob providing the extra muscle. It took four round-trips to transfer the bulk of the stuff from Alexandra Road, and at the end of the day there was still a good deal of bric-a-brac left behind, to be collected at a later point.

About two in the afternoon, Kirsty turned up on the doorstep.

"Came to see if I could give you a hand," she said, with a tone of vague apology in her voice.

"Well, you'd better come in," Julia said.

She went back into the front room, which was a battlefield in which only chaos was winning, and quietly cursed Rory. Inviting the lost soul round to offer her services was his doing, no doubt of it. She would be more of a hindrance than a help; her dreamy, perpetually defeated manner set Julia's teeth on edge.

"What can I do?" Kirsty asked. "Rory said—"

"Yes," said Julia. "I'm sure he did."

"Where is he? Rory, I mean."

"Gone back for another vanload, to add to the misery."

"Oh."

Julia softened her expression. "You know it's very sweet of you," she said, "to come round like this, but I don't think there's much you can do just at the moment."

Kirsty flushed slightly. Dreamy she was, but not stupid.

"I see," she said. "Are you sure? Can't . . . I mean, maybe I could make a cup of coffee for you?"

"Coffee," said Julia. The thought of it made her realize just how parched her throat had become. "Yes," she conceded. "That's not a bad idea."

The coffeemaking was not without its

minor traumas. No task Kirsty undertook was ever entirely simple. She stood in the kitchen, boiling water in a pan it had taken a quarter of an hour to find, thinking that maybe she shouldn't have come after all. Julia always looked at her so strangely, as if faintly baffled by the fact that she hadn't been smothered at birth. No matter. *Rory* had asked her to come, hadn't he? And that was invitation enough. She would not have turned down the chance of his smile for a hundred Julias.

The van arrived twenty-five minutes later, minutes in which the women had twice attempted, and twice failed, to get a conversation simmering. They had little in common. Julia the sweet, the beautiful, the winner of glances and kisses, and Kirsty the girl with the pale handshake, whose eyes were only ever as bright as Julia's before or after tears. She had long ago decided that life was unfair. But why, when she'd accepted that bitter truth, did circumstance insist on rubbing her face in it?

She surreptitiously watched Julia as she worked, and it seemed to Kirsty that the woman was incapable of ugliness. Every gesture—a stray hair brushed from the eyes with the back of the hand, dust blown from a favorite cup—all were infused with such effortless grace. Seeing it, she understood Rory's doglike adulation, and understanding it, despaired afresh.

He came in, at last, squinting and sweaty. The afternoon sun was fierce. He grinned at her, parading the ragged line of his front teeth that she had first found so irresistible.

"I'm glad you could come," he said.

"Happy to help—" she replied, but he had already looked away, at Julia.

"How's it going?"

"I'm losing my mind," she told him.

"Well, now you can rest from your labors," he said. "We brought the bed this trip." He gave her a conspiratorial wink, but she didn't respond.

"Can I help with unloading?" Kirsty offered.

"Lewton and M.B. are doing it," came Rory's reply.

"Oh."

"But I'd give an arm and a leg for a cup of tea."

"We haven't found the tea," Julia told him.

"Oh. Maybe a coffee, then?"

"Right," said Kirsty. "And for the other two?"

"They'd kill for a cup."

Kirsty went back to the kitchen, filled the small pan to near brimming, and set it back on the stove. From the hallway she heard Rory supervising the next unloading.

It was the bed, the bridal bed. Though she tried very hard to keep the thought of his embracing Julia out of her mind, she could not. As she stared into the water, and it simmered and steamed and finally boiled, the same painful images of their pleasure came back and back.

3

While the trio were away, gathering the fourth and final load of the day, Julia lost her temper with the unpacking. It was a disaster, she said; everything had been parceled up and put into the tea chests in the wrong order. She was having to disinter perfectly useless items to get access to the bare necessities.

Kirsty kept her silence, and her place in the kitchen, washing the soiled cups.

Cursing louder, Julia left the chaos and went out for a cigarette on the front step. She leaned against the open door, and breathed the pollen-gilded air. Already, though it was only the twenty-first of August, the afternoon was tinged with a smoky scent that heralded autumn.

She had lost track of how fast the day had gone, for as she stood there a bell began to ring for Evensong: the run of chimes rising and falling in lazy waves. The sound was reassuring. It made her think of her childhood, though not—that she could remember—of any particular day or place. Simply of being young, of mystery.

It was four years since she'd last stepped into a church: the day of her marriage to Rory, in fact. The thought of that day—or rather, of the promise it had failed to fulfill—soured the moment. She left the step, the chimes in full flight, and turned back into the house. After the touch of the sun on her upturned face, the interior seemed gloomy. Suddenly she tired to the point of tears.

They would have to assemble the bed before they could put their heads down to sleep tonight, and they had yet to decide which room they would use as the master bedroom. She would do that now, she elected, and so avoid having to return to the front room, and to ever-mournful Kirsty.

The bell was still pealing when she opened

the door of the front room on the second floor. It was the largest of the three upper rooms—a natural choice—but the sun had not got in today (or any other day this summer) because the blinds were drawn across the window. The room was consequently chillier than anywhere else in the house; the air stagnant. She crossed the stained floorboards to the window, intending to remove the blind.

At the sill, a strange thing. The blind had been securely *nailed* to the window frame, effectively cutting out the least intrusion of life from the sunlit street beyond. She tried to pull the material free, but failed. The workman, whoever he'd been, had done a thorough job.

No matter; she'd have Rory take a claw hammer to the nails when he got back. She turned from the window, and as she did so she was suddenly and forcibly aware that the bell was still summoning the faithful. Were they not coming tonight? Was the hook not sufficiently baited with promises of paradise? The thought was only half alive; it withered in moments. But the bell rolled on, reverberating around the room. Her limbs, already aching with fatigue, seemed dragged down further by each peal. Her head throbbed intolerably.

The room was hateful, she'd decided; it

was stale, and its benighted walls clammy. Despite its size, she would not let Rory persuade her into using it as the master bedroom. Let it rot.

She started toward the door, but as she came within a yard of it, the corners of the room seemed to creak, and the door slammed. Her nerves jangled. It was all she could do to prevent herself from sobbing.

Instead she simply said, "Go to hell," and snatched at the handle. It turned easily (why should it not? yet she was relieved) and the door swung open. From the hall below, a splash of warmth and ocher light.

She closed the door behind her and, with a queer satisfaction the root of which she couldn't or wouldn't fathom turned the key in the lock.

As she did so, the bell stopped.

-------------------- 4 --------------------

"But it's the biggest of the rooms . . ."

"I don't like it, Rory. It's damp. We can use the back room."

"If we can get the bloody bed through the door."

"Of course we can. You know we can."

"Seems a waste of a good room," he protested, knowing full well that this was a *fait accompli.*

"Mother knows best," she told him, and smiled at him with eyes whose luster was far from maternal.

THREE

*T*he seasons long for each other, like men and women, in order that they may be cured of their excesses.

Spring, if it lingers more than a week beyond its span, starts to hunger for summer to end the days of perpetual promise. Summer in its turn soon begins to sweat for something to quench its heat, and the mellowest of autumns will tire of gentility at last, and ache for a quick sharp frost to kill its fruitfulness.

Even winter—the hardest season, the most implacable—dreams, as February creeps on, of the flame that will presently melt it away. Everything tires with time, and starts to seek some opposition, to save it from itself.

So August gave way to September and there were few complaints.

2

With work, the house on Lodovico Street began to look more hospitable. There were even visits from neighbors, who—after sizing up the couple—spoke freely of how happy they were to have number fifty-five occupied again. Only one of them made any mention of Frank, referring in passing to the odd fellow who'd lived in the house for a few weeks the previous summer. There was a moment of embarrassment when Rory revealed the tenant to have been his brother, but it was soon glossed over by Julia, whose power to charm knew no bounds.

Rory had seldom made mention of Frank during the years of his marriage to Julia, though he and his brother were only eighteen months apart in age, and had, as children, been inseparable. This Julia had learned on an occasion of drunken reminiscing—a month or two before the wedding—when Rory had spoken at length about Frank. It had been melancholy talk. The brothers' paths had diverged considerably once they'd passed through adolescence, and Rory regretted it. Regretted still more the pain Frank's wild life-style had brought to their parents. It seemed that when Frank appeared, once in a blue moon, from whichever corner of the globe he was presently laying waste, he only brought grief. His tales of adventures in the shallows of criminality, his talk of whores and petty theft, all appalled their parents. But there had been worse, or so Rory had said. In his wilder moments Frank had talked of a life lived in delirium, of an appetite for experience that conceded no moral imperative.

Was it the tone of Rory's telling, a mixture of revulsion and envy, that had so piqued Julia's curiosity? Whatever the reason, she had been quickly seized by an unquenchable curiosity concerning this madman.

Then, barely a fortnight before the wedding, the black sheep had appeared in the flesh. Things had gone well for him of late. He was wearing gold rings on his fingers, and his skin was tight and tanned. There was little outward sign of the monster Rory had described. Brother Frank was smooth as a polished stone. She had succumbed to his charm within hours.

A strange time ensued. As the days crept toward the date of the wedding she found herself thinking less and less of her husband-to-be, and more and more of his brother. They were not wholly dissimilar; a certain lilt in their voices, and their easy manner, marked them as siblings. But to Rory's qualities Frank brought something his brother would never have: a beautiful desperation.

Perhaps what had happened next had been inevitable; and no matter how hard she'd fought her instincts, she would only have postponed the consummation of their feelings for each other. At least that was how she tried to excuse herself later. But when all the self-recrimination was done with, she still treasured the memory of their first—and last—encounter.

Kirsty had been at the house, hadn't she?, on some matrimonial business, when Frank had arrived. But by that telepathy that comes with desire (and fades with it) Julia had known that today was the day. She'd left Kirsty to her listmaking or suchlike, and taken Frank upstairs on the pretext of showing him the wed-

ding dress. That was how she remembered it—
that he'd asked to see the dress—and she'd put
the veil on, laughing to think of herself in
white, and then he'd been at her shoulder,
lifting the veil, and she'd laughed on, laughed
and laughed, as though to test the strength of
his purpose. He had not been cooled by her
mirth however; nor had he wasted time with
the niceties of a seduction. The smooth exte-
rior gave way to cruder stuff almost immediately. Their coupling had had in every regard
but the matter of her acquiescence, all the ag-
gression and the joylessness of rape.

Memory sweetened events of course, and
in the four years (and five months) since that
afternoon, she'd replayed the scene often.
Now, in remembering it, the bruises were tro-
phies of their passion, her tears proof positive
of her feelings for him.

The day following, he'd disappeared. Flitted off to Bangkok or Easter Island, some place
where he had no debts to answer. She'd
mourned him, couldn't help it. Nor had her
mourning gone unnoticed. Though it was
never explicitly discussed, she had often wondered if the subsequent deterioration of her
relationship with Rory had not started there:

with her thinking of Frank as she made love to his brother.

And now? Now, despite the change of domestic interiors, and the chance of a fresh start together, it seemed that events conspired to remind her again of Frank.

It wasn't just the gossip of the neighbors that brought him to mind. One day, when she was alone in the house and unpacking various personal belongings, she came across several wallets of Rory's photographs. Many were relatively recent: pictures of the two of them together in Athens and Malta. But buried amongst the transparent smiles were some pictures she couldn't remember ever having seen before (had Rory kept them from her?); family portraits that went back decades. A photograph of his parents on their wedding day, the black and white image eroded over the years to a series of grays. Pictures of christenings, in which proud godparents cradled babies smothered in the family lace.

And then, photographs of the brothers together; as toddlers, with wide eyes; as surly schoolchildren, snapped at gymnastic displays and in school pageants. Then, as the shyness of acne-ridden adolescence took over, the number of pictures dwindled—until the frogs emerged, as princes, the other side of puberty.

Seeing Frank in brilliant color, clowning for the camera, she felt herself blushing. He had been an exhibitionist youth, predictably enough, always dressed *à la mode*. Rory, by comparison, looked dowdy. It seemed to her that the brothers' future lives were sketched in these early portraits. Frank the smiling, seductive chameleon; Rory the solid citizen.

She had packed the pictures away at last, and found, when she stood up, that with the blushes had come tears. Not of regret. She had no use for that. It was *fury* that made her eyes sting. Somehow, between one breath and the next, she'd lost herself.

She knew too, with perfect certainty, when her grip had first faltered. Lying on a bed of wedding lace, while Frank beset her neck with kisses.

3

Once in a while she went up to the room with the sealed blinds.

So far, they'd done little decorating work on the upper floors, preferring to first organize

the areas in public gaze. The room had therefore remained untouched. *Unentered*, indeed,
except for these few visits of hers.

She wasn't sure why she went up, nor how
to account for the odd assortment of feelings
that beset her while there. But there was something about the dark interior that gave her
comfort; it was a womb of sorts, a dead
woman's womb. Sometimes, when Rory was at
work, she simply took herself up the stairs and
sat in the stillness, thinking of nothing; or at
least nothing she could put words to.

These sojourns made her feel oddly guilty,
and she tried to stay away from the room when
Rory was around. But it wasn't always possible.
Sometimes her feet took her there without instruction to do so.

It happened thus that Saturday, the day of
the blood.

She had been watching Rory at work on
the kitchen door, chiseling several layers of
paint from around the hinges, when she
seemed to hear the room call. Satisfied that he
was thoroughly engrossed in his chores, she
went upstairs.

It was cooler than usual, and she was glad
of it. She put her hand to the wall, and then
transferred her chilled palm to her forehead.

"No use," she murmured to herself, picturing the man at work downstairs. She didn't love him; no more than he, beneath his infatuation with her face, loved her. He chiseled in a world of his own; she suffered here, far removed from him.

A gust of wind caught the back door below. She heard it slam.

Downstairs, the sound made Rory lose his concentration. The chisel jumped its groove and sliced deeply into the thumb of his left hand. He shouted, as a gush of color came. The chisel hit the floor.

"Hell and damnation!"

She heard, but did nothing. Too late, she surfaced through a stupor of melancholy to realize that he was coming upstairs. Fumbling for the key, and an excuse to justify her presence in the room, she stood up, but he was already at the door, crossing the threshold, rushing toward her, his right hand clamped ineptly around his left. Blood was coming in abundance. It welled up between his fingers and dribbled down his arm, dripping from his elbow, adding stain to stain on the bare boards.

"What have you done?" she asked him.

"What does it look like?" he said through gritted teeth. "Cut myself."

His face and neck had gone the color of window putty. She'd seen him like this before; he had on occasion passed out at the sight of his own blood.

"Do something," he said queasily.

"Is it deep?"

"I don't know!" he yelled at her. "I don't want to look."

He was ridiculous, she thought, but this wasn't the time to give vent to the contempt she felt. Instead she took his bloody hand in hers and, while he looked away, prized the palm from the cut. It was sizable, and still bleeding profusely. Deep blood, dark blood.

"I think we'd better take you off to the hospital," she told him.

"Can you cover it up?" he asked, his voice devoid of anger now.

"Sure. I'll get a clean binding. Come on—"

"No," he said, shaking his ashen face. "If I take a step, I think I'll pass out."

"Stay here then," she soothed him. "You'll be fine."

Finding no bandages in the bathroom cabinet the equal of the staunching, she fetched a few clean handkerchiefs from his drawer and went back into the room. He was leaning against the wall now, his skin glossy with sweat. He had padded in the blood he'd shed; she could taste the tang of it in the air.

Still quietly reassuring him that he wouldn't die of a two-inch cut, she wound a handkerchief around his hand, bound it on with a second, then escorted him, trembling like a leaf, down the stairs (one by one, like a child) and out to the car.

At the hospital they waited an hour in a queue of the walking wounded before he was finally seen, and stitched up. It was difficult for her to know in retrospect what was more comical about the episode: his weakness, or the extravagance of his subsequent gratitude. She told him, when he became fulsome, that she didn't want thanks from him, and it was true.

She wanted nothing that he could offer her, except perhaps his absence.

4

"Did you clean up the floor in the damp room?" she asked him the following day. They'd called it the damp room since that first Sunday, though there was not a sign of rot from ceiling to skirting board.

Rory looked up from his magazine. Gray moons hung beneath his eyes. He hadn't slept well, so he'd said. A cut finger, and he had nightmares of mortality. She, on the other hand, had slept like a babe.

"What did you say?" he asked her.

"The floor—" she said again. "There was blood on the floor. You cleaned it up."

He shook his head. "No," he said simply and returned to the magazine.

"Well I didn't," she said.

He offered her an indulgent smile. "You're such a perfect hausfrau," he said. "You don't even know when you're doing it."

The subject was closed there. He was content, apparently, to believe that she was quietly losing her sanity.

She, on the other hand, had the strangest sense that she was about to find it again.

FOUR

*K*irsty hated parties. The smiles to be pasted on over the panic, the glances to be interpreted, and worst, the conversation. She had nothing to say of the least interest to the world, of this she had long been convinced. She'd watched too many eyes glaze over to believe otherwise, seen every device known to man for wheedling oneself out of the company of the dull, from "Will you excuse me, I believe I see my accountant," to passing out dead drunk at her feet.

But Rory had insisted she come to the housewarming. Just a few close friends, he'd promised. She'd said yes, knowing all too well what scenario would ensue from refusal. Moping at home in a stew of self-recrimination, cursing her cowardice, and thinking of Rory's sweet face.

The gathering wasn't such a torment as it turned out. There were only nine guests *in toto*, all of whom she knew vaguely, which made it easier. They didn't expect her to illuminate the room, only to nod and laugh where appropriate. And Rory—his hand still bound up—was at his most winning, full of guileless bonhomie. She even wondered if Neville—one of Rory's work colleagues—wasn't making eyes at her behind his spectacles, a suspicion that was confirmed in the middle of the evening when he maneuvered himself to her side and inquired whether she had any interest in cat breeding. She told him she hadn't, but was always interested in new experiences. He seemed delighted, and on this fragile pretext proceeded to ply her with liqueurs for the rest of the night. By eleven-thirty she was a whoozy but happy wreck, prompted by the most casual remark to ever more painful fits of giggling.

A little after midnight, Julia declared that she was tired, and wanted to go to bed. The statement was taken as a general cue for dispersal, but Rory would have none of it. He was up and refilling glasses before anyone had a chance to protest. Kirsty was certain she caught a look of displeasure cross Julia's face, then it passed, and the brow was unsullied once again. She said her good-nights, was complimented profusely on her skill with calf's liver, and went to bed.

The flawlessly beautiful were flawlessly happy, weren't they? To Kirsty this had always seemed self-evident. Tonight, however, the alcohol made her wonder if envy hadn't blinded her. Perhaps to be flawless was another kind of sadness.

But her spinning head had an inept hold on such ruminations, and the next minute Rory was up, and telling a joke about a gorilla and a Jesuit that had her choking on her drink before he'd even got to the votive candles.

Upstairs, Julia heard a fresh bout of laughter. She was indeed tired, as she'd claimed, but it wasn't the cooking that had exhausted her. It was the effort of suppressing her contempt for the damn fools who were gathered in the lounge below. She'd called them friends once, these half-wits, with their poor jokes and their poorer pretensions. She had played along with them for several hours; it was enough. Now she needed some cool place, some darkness.

As soon as she opened the door of the damp room she knew things were not quite as they had been. The light from the shadeless bulb on the landing illuminated the boards where Rory's blood had fallen, now so clean they might have been scrubbed. Beyond the reach of the light, the room bowed to darkness. She stepped in, and closed the door. The lock clicked into place at her back.

The dark was almost perfect, and she was glad of it. Her eyes rested against the night, their surfaces chilled.

Then, from the far side of the room, she heard a sound.

It was no louder than the din of a cockroach running behind the skirting boards. After seconds, it stopped. She held her breath. It came again. This time there seemed to be some pattern to the sound; a primitive code.

They were laughing like loons downstairs. The noise awoke desperation in her. What would she not do, to be free of such company?

She swallowed, and spoke to the darkness. "I hear you," she said, not certain of why the words came, or to whom they were addressed.

The cockroach scratches ceased for a moment, and then began again, more urgently. She stepped away from the door and moved toward the noise. It continued, as if summoning her.

It was easy to miscalculate in the dark, and she reached the wall before she'd expected to. Raising her hands, she began to run her palms over the painted plaster. The surface was not uniformly cold. There was a place, she judged it to be halfway between door and window, where the chill became so intense she had to break contact. The cockroach stopped scratching.

There was a moment when she swam, totally disoriented, in darkness and silence. And then, something moved in front of her. A trick of her mind's eye, she assumed, for there was only imagined light to be had here. But the next spectacle showed her the error of that assumption.

The wall was alight, or rather something behind it burned with a cold luminescence that made the solid brick seem insubstantial stuff.

More; the wall seemed to be coming apart, segments of it shifting and dislocating like a magician's prop, oiled panels giving on to hidden boxes whose sides in turn collapsed to reveal some further hiding place. She watched fixedly, not daring to even blink for fear she miss some detail of this extraordinary sleight-of-hand, while pieces of the world came apart in front of her eyes.

Then, suddenly, somewhere in this ever more elaborate system of sliding fragments, she saw (or again, *seemed* to see) movement. Only now did she realize that she'd been holding her breath since this display began, and was beginning to become light-headed. She tried to empty her lungs of the stale air, and take a draught of fresh, but her body would not obey this simple instruction.

Somewhere in her innards a tic of panic began. The hocus-pocus had stopped now, leaving one part of her admiring quite dispassionately the tinkling music that was coming from the wall, the other part fighting the fear that rose in her throat step by step.

Again, she tried to take a breath, but it was as if her body had died, and she was staring out of it, unable now to breathe or blink or swallow.

The spectacle of the unfolding wall had now ceased entirely, and she saw something flicker across the brick, ragged enough to be shadow but too substantial.

It was human, she saw, or had been. But the body had been ripped apart and sewn together again with most of its pieces either missing or twisted and blackened as if in a furnace. There was an eye, gleaming at her, and the ladder of a spine, the vertebrae stripped of muscle, a few unrecognizable fragments of anatomy. That was it. That such a thing might live beggared reason—what little flesh it owned was hopelessly corrupted. Yet live it did. Its eye, despite the rot it was rooted in, scanned her every inch, up and down.

She felt no fear in its presence. This thing was weaker than her by far. It moved a little in its cell, looking for some modicum of comfort. But there was none to be had, not for a creature that wore its frayed nerves on its bleeding sleeve. Every place it might lay its body brought pain: this she knew indisputably. She pitied it. And with pity came release. Her body expelled dead air, and sucked in living. Her oxygen-starved brain reeled.

Even as she did so it spoke, a hole opening

up in the flayed ball of the monster's head and issued a single, weightless word.

The word was:

"Julia."

Kirsty put down her glass, and tried to stand up.

"Where are you going?" Neville asked her.

"Where do you think?" she replied, consciously trying to prevent the words from slurring.

"Do you need any help?" Rory inquired. The alcohol made his lids lazy, and his grin lazier still.

"I am house-trained," she replied, the riposte greeted with laughter all around. She was pleased with herself; off-the-cuff wit was not her forte. She stumbled to the door.

"It's the last room on the right at the end of the landing," Rory informed her.

"I know," she said, and stepped out into the hall.

She didn't usually enjoy the sensation of drunkenness, but tonight she was reveling in it.

She felt loose-limbed and light-hearted. She might well regret this tomorrow, but tomorrow would have to take care of itself. For tonight, she was flying.

She found her way to the bathroom, and relieved her aching bladder, then splashed some water onto her face. That done, she began her return journey.

She had taken three steps along the landing when she realized that somebody had put out the landing light while she was in the bathroom, and that same somebody was now standing a few yards away from her. She stopped.

"Hello?" she said. Had the cat breeder followed her upstairs, in the hope of proving he wasn't spayed?

"Is that you?" she asked, only dimly aware that this was a singularly fruitless line of inquiry.

There was no reply, and she became a little uneasy.

"Come on," she said, attempting a jocular manner that she hoped masked her anxiety, "who is it?"

"Me," said Julia. Her voice was odd. Throaty, perhaps tearful.

"Are you all right?" Kirsty asked her. She wished she could see Julia's face.

"Yes," came the reply. "Why shouldn't I be?" Within the space of those five words the actress in Julia seized control. The voice cleared, the tone lightened.

"I'm just tired . . ." she went on. "It sounds like you're having a good time down there."

"Are we keeping you awake?"

"Goodness me, no," the voice gushed, "I was just going to the bathroom." A pause; then: "You go back down. Enjoy yourself."

At this cue Kirsty moved toward her along the landing. At the last possible moment Julia stepped out of the way, avoiding even the slightest physical contact.

"Sleep well," Kirsty said at the top of the stairs.

But there was no reply forthcoming from the shadow on the landing.

3

Julia didn't sleep well. Not that night, nor any night that followed.

What she'd seen in the damp room, what she'd heard and, finally, *felt*—was enough to keep easy slumbers at bay forever, or so she began to believe.

He was here. Brother Frank was here, in the house—and had been all the time. Locked away from the world in which she lived and breathed, but close enough to make the frail, pitiful contact he had. The whys and the wherefores of this she had no clue to; the human detritus in the wall had neither the strength nor the time to articulate its condition.

All it said, before the wall began to close on it again, and its wreckage was once more eclipsed by brick and plaster, was *"Julia"*— then, simply: *"It's Frank"*—and at the very end the word *"Blood."*

Then it was gone completely, and her legs had given way beneath her. She'd half fallen, half staggered, backward against the opposite wall. By the time she gathered her wits about her once more there was no mysterious light, no wasted figure cocooned in the brick. Reality's hold was absolute once again.

Not *quite* absolute perhaps. Frank was still here, in the damp room. Of that she had no doubt. Out of sight he might be, but not out of mind. He was trapped somehow between the sphere she occupied and some other place:

a place of bells and troubled darkness. Had he died? Was that it? Perished in the empty room the previous summer, and now awaiting exorcism? If so, what had happened to his earthly remains? Only further exchange with Frank himself, or the remnants thereof, would provide an explanation.

Of the means by which she could lend the lost soul strength she had little doubt. He had given her the solution plainly.

"Blood," he'd said. The syllable had been spoken not as an accusation but as an imperative.

Rory had bled on the floor of the damp room; the splashes had subsequently disappeared. Somehow, Frank's ghost—if that it was—had fed upon his brother's spillage, and gained thereby nourishment enough to reach out from his cell, and make faltering contact. What more might be achieved if the supply were larger?

She thought of Frank's embraces, of his roughness, his hardness, of the insistence he had brought to bear upon her. What would she not give to have such insistence again? Perhaps it was possible. And if it were—if she could give him the sustenance he needed—would he not be grateful? Would he not be her pet, docile or brutal at her least whim? The thought took sleep away. Took sanity and sorrow with it. She had been in love all this time, she realized, and mourning for him. If it took blood to restore him to her, then blood she would supply, and not think twice of the consequences.

In the days that followed, she found her smile again. Rory took the change of mood as a sign that she was happy in the new house. Her good humor ignited the same in him. He took to the redecoration with renewed gusto.

Soon, he said, he would get to work on the second floor. They would locate the source of dampness in the large room, and turn it into a bedroom fit for his princess. She kissed his cheek when he spoke of this, and she said that she was in no hurry, that the room they had already was more than adequate. Talk of the bedroom made him stroke her neck, and pull her close, and whisper infantile obscenities in her ear. She did not refuse him, but went upstairs meekly, and let him undress her as he liked to do, unbuttoning her with paint-stained fingers. She pretended the ceremony aroused her, though this was far from the truth.

The only thing that sparked the least appetite in her, as she lay on the creaking bed with his bulk between her legs, was closing her eyes and picturing Frank, as he had been.

More than once his name rose to her lips; each time she bit it back. Finally she opened her eyes to remind herself of the boorish truth. Rory was decorating her face with his kisses. Her cheeks crawled at his touch.

She would not be able to endure this too often, she realized. It was too much of an effort to play the acquiescent wife: her heart would burst.

Thus, lying beneath him while September's breath brushed her face from the open window, she began to plot the getting of blood.

FIVE

*S*ometimes it seemed that eons came and went while he lingered in the wall, eons that some clue would later reveal to have been the passing of hours, or even minutes.

But now things had changed; he had a chance of *escape*. His spirit soared at the thought. It was a frail chance, he didn't deceive himself about that. There were several reasons his best efforts might falter. Julia, for one. He remembered her as a trite, preening woman, whose upbringing had curbed her capacity for passion. He had untamed her, of course, once. He remembered the day, among the thousands of times he had performed that act, with some satisfaction. She had resisted no more than was needful for her vanity, then succumbed with such naked fervor he had almost lost control of himself.

In other circumstances he might have snatched her from under her would-be husband's nose, but fraternal politics counseled otherwise. In a week or two he would have tired of her, and been left not only with a woman whose body was already an eyesore to him, but also a vengeful brother on his heels. It hadn't been worth the hassle.

Besides, there'd been new worlds to conquer. He had left the day after to go East: to Hong King and Sri Lanka, to wealth and adventure. He'd had them, too. At least for a while. But everything slipped through his fingers sooner or later, and with time he began to wonder whether it was circumstance that denied him a good hold on his earnings, or whether he simply didn't care enough to keep what he had. The train of thought, once begun, was a runaway. Everywhere, in the wreckage around him, he found evidence to support the same bitter thesis: that he had encountered nothing in his life—no person, no state of mind or body—he wanted sufficiently to suffer even passing discomfort for.

A downward spiral began. He spent three months in a wash of depression and self-pity that bordered on the suicidal. But even that solution was denied him by his newfound nihilism. If nothing was worth living for it followed, didn't it, that there was nothing worth dying for either. He stumbled from one such sterility to the next, until all thoughts were rotted away by whatever opiate his immoralities could earn him.

How had he first heard about Lemarchand's box? He couldn't remember. In a bar maybe, or a gutter, from the lips of a fellow derelict. At the time it was merely a rumor—this dream of a pleasure dome where those who had exhausted the trivial delights of the human condition might discover a fresh definition of joy. And the route to this paradise? There were several, he was told, charts of the interface between the real and the realer still, made by travelers whose bones had long since gone to dust. One such chart was in the vaults of the Vatican, hidden in code in a theological work unread since the Reformation. Another—in the form of an origami exercise, was reported to have been in the possession of the Marquis de Sade, who used it, while imprisoned in the Bastille, to barter with a guard for paper on which to write *The 120 Days of Sodom.* Yet another was made by a craftsman—a maker of singing birds—called Lemarchand, in the form of a musical box of such elaborate design a man might toy with it half a lifetime and never get inside.

Stories. Stories. Yet since he had come to believe in nothing at all it was not so difficult to put the tyranny of verifiable truth out of his head. And it passed the time, musing drunkenly on such fantasies.

It was in Düsseldorf, where he'd gone smuggling heroin, that he again encountered the story of Lemarchand's box. His curiosity was piqued once more, but this time he followed the story up until he found its source. The man's name was Kircher, though he probably laid claim to half a dozen others. Yes, the German could confirm the existence of the box, and yes, he could see his way to letting Frank have it. The price? Small favors, here and there. Nothing exceptional. Frank did the favors, washed his hands, and claimed his payment.

There had been instructions from Kircher, on how best to break the seal on Lemarchand's device, instructions that were part pragmatic, part metaphysical. To solve the puzzle is to travel, he'd said, or something like that. The box, it seemed, was not just the map of the road, but the road itself.

This new addiction quickly cured him of dope and drink. Perhaps there were other ways to bend the world to suit the shape of his dreams.

He came back to the house on Lodovico Street, to the empty house behind whose walls he was now imprisoned, and prepared himself—just as Kircher had detailed—for the challenge of solving Lemarchand's Configuration. He had never in his life been so abstemious, nor so single-minded. In the days before the onslaught on the box he led a life that would have shamed a saint, focusing all his energies on the ceremonies ahead.

He had been arrogant in his dealing with the Order of the Gash, he saw that now; but there were everywhere—*in* the world and *out* of it—forces that encouraged such arrogance because they traded on it. That in itself would not have undone him. No, his real error had been the naive belief that *his* definition of pleasure significantly overlapped with that of the Cenobites.

As it was, they had brought incalculable suffering. They had overdosed him on sensuality, until his mind teetered on madness, then they'd initiated him into experiences that his nerves still convulsed to recall. They had called it pleasure, and perhaps they'd meant it. Perhaps not. It was impossible to know with these minds; they were so hopelessly, flawlessly ambiguous. They recognized no principles of reward and punishment by which he could hope to win some respite from their tortures, nor were they touched by any appeal for mercy. He'd tried that, over the weeks and months that separated the solving of the box from today.

There was no compassion to be had on this side of the Schism; there was only the weeping and the laughter. Tears of joy sometimes (for an hour without dread, a breath's length even), laughter coming just as paradoxically in the face of some new horror, fashioned by the Engineer for the provision of grief.

There was a further sophistication to the torture, devised by a mind that understood exquisitely the nature of suffering. The prisoners were allowed to see into the world they had once occupied. Their resting places—when they were not enduring pleasure—looked out onto the very locations where they had once worked the Configuration that had brought them here. In Frank's case, onto the upper room of number fifty-five, Lodovico Street.

For the best part of a year it had been an unilluminating view: nobody had ever stepped into the house. And then, *they'd* come: Rory and the lovely Julia. And hope had begun again. . . .

There were ways to escape, he'd heard it whispered; loopholes in the system that might allow a mind supple or cunning enough egress into the room from which it had come. If a prisoner were able to make such an escape, there was no way that the hierophants could follow. They had to be *summoned* across the Schism. Without such an invitation they were left like dogs on the doorstep, scratching and scratching but unable to get in. Escape therefore, if it could be achieved, brought with it a *decree absolute*, total dissolution of the mistaken marriage which the prisoner had made. It was a risk worth taking. Indeed it was no risk at all. What punishment could be meted out worse than the thought of pain without hope of release?

He had been lucky. Some prisoners had departed from the world without leaving sufficient sign of themselves from which, given an adequate collision of circumstances, their bodies might be remade. He had. Almost his last act, bar the shouting, had been to empty his testicles onto the floor. Dead sperm was a meager keepsake of his essential self, but enough. When dear brother Rory (sweet butterfingered Rory) had let his chisel slip, there was something of Frank to profit from the pain. He had found a fingerhold for himself, and a glimpse of strength with which he might haul himself to safety. Now it was up to Julia.

Sometimes, suffering in the wall, he thought she would desert him out of fear. Either that or she'd rationalize the vision she'd seen, and decide she'd been dreaming. If so, he was lost. He lacked the energy to repeat the appearance.

But there were signs that gave him cause for hope. The fact that she returned to the room on two or three occasions, for instance, and simply stood in the gloom, watching the wall. She'd even muttered a few words on the second visit, though he'd caught only scraps. The word *"here"* was amongst them. And *"waiting,"* and *"soon."* Enough to keep him from despair.

He had another prop to his optimism. She was lost, wasn't she? He'd seen that in her face, when—before the day Rory had chiseled himself—she and his brother had had occasion to be in the room together. He'd read the looks between the lines, the moments when her guard had slipped, and the sadness and frustration she felt were apparent.

Yes, she was lost. Married to a man she felt no love for, and unable to see a way out.

Well, here he was. They could save each other, the way the poets promised lovers should. He was mystery, he was darkness, he was all she had dreamed of. And if she would only free him he would service her—oh yes—until her pleasure reached that threshold that, like all thresholds, was a place where the strong grew stronger, and the weak perished.

Pleasure was pain there, and vice versa. And he knew it well enough to call it home.

SIX

It turned cold in the third week of September: an Arctic chill brought on a rapacious wind that stripped the trees of leaves in a handful of days.

The cold necessitated a change of costume, and a change of plan. Instead of walking, Julia took the car. Drove down to the city center in the early afternoon and found a bar in which the lunchtime trade was brisk but not clamorous.

The customers came and went: Young Turks from firms of lawyers and accountants, debating their ambitions; parties of wine-imbibers whose only claim to sobriety was their suits; and, more interestingly, a smattering of individuals who sat alone at their tables and simply drank. She garnered a good crop of admiring glances, but they were mostly from the Young Turks. It wasn't until she'd been in the place an hour, and the wage slaves were returning to their treadmills, that she caught sight of somebody watching her reflection in the bar mirror. For the next ten minutes his eyes were glued to her. She went on drinking, trying to conceal any sign of agitation. And then, without warning, he stood up and crossed to her table.

"Drinking alone?" he said.

She wanted to run. Her heart was pounding so furiously she was certain he must hear it. But no. He asked her if she wanted another drink; she said she did. Clearly pleased not to have been rebuffed, he went to the bar, ordered doubles, and returned to her side. He was ruddy-featured, and one size larger than his dark blue suit. Only his eyes betrayed any sign of nervousness, resting on her for moments only, then darting away like startled fish.

There would be no serious conversation: that she had already decided. She didn't want to know much about him. His name, if necessary. His profession and marital status, if he insisted. Beyond that let him be just a body.

As it was there was no danger of a confessional. She'd met more talkative paving stones. He smiled occasionally—a short, nervous smile that showed teeth too even to be real—and offered more drinks. She said no, wanting the chase over with as soon as possible, and instead asked if he had time for a coffee. He said he had.

"The house is only a few minutes from here," she replied, and they went to her car. She kept wondering, as she drove—the meat on the seat beside her—why this was so very easy. Was it that the man was plainly a victim—with his ineffectual eyes and his artificial teeth—born, did he but know it, to make this journey? Yes, perhaps that was it. She was not afraid, because all of this was so perfectly predictable. . . .

As she turned the key in the front door and stepped into the house, she thought she heard a noise in the kitchen. Had Rory returned home early, ill perhaps? She called out.

There was no reply; the house was empty. Almost.

From the threshold on, she had the thing planned meticulously. She closed the door. The man in the blue suit stared at his manicured hands, and waited for his cue.

"I get lonely sometimes," she told him as she brushed past him. It was a line she'd come up with in bed the previous night.

He only nodded by way of response, the expression on his face a mingling of fear and incredulity: he clearly couldn't quite believe his luck.

"Do you want another drink?" she asked him, "or shall we go straight upstairs?"

He only nodded again.

"Which?"

"I think maybe I've drunk enough already."

"Upstairs then."

He made an indecisive move in her direction, as though he might have intended a kiss. She wanted no courtship, however. Skirting his touch, she crossed to the bottom of the stairs.

"I'll lead," she said. Meekly, he followed.

At the top of the steps she glanced round at him, and caught him dabbing sweat from his chin with his handkerchief. She waited until he caught up with her, and then led him halfway along the landing to the damp room.

The door had been left ajar.

"Come on in," she said.

He obeyed. Once inside it took him a few moments to become accustomed to the gloom, and a further time to give voice to his observation: "There's no bed."

She closed the door, and switched on the light. She had hung one of Rory's old jackets on the back of the door. In its pocket she'd left the knife.

He said again: "No bed."

"What's wrong with the floor?" she replied.

"The floor?"

"Take off your jacket. You're warm."

"I am," he agreed, but did nothing, so she moved across to him, and began to slip the knot of his tie. He was trembling, poor lamb. Poor, bleatless lamb. While she removed the tie, he began to shrug off his jacket.

Was Frank watching this? she wondered. Her eyes strayed momentarily to the wall. Yes, she thought; he's there. He *sees*. He *knows*. He licks his lips and grows impatient.

The lamb spoke. "Why don't you . . ." he

began, "why don't you maybe . . . do the same?"

"Would you like to see me naked?" she teased. The words made his eyes gleam.

"Yes," he said thickly. "Yes. I'd like that."

"Very much?"

"Very much."

He was unbuttoning his shirt.

"Maybe you will," she said.

He gave her that dwarf smile again.

"Is it a game?" he ventured.

"If you want it to be," she said, and helped him out of his shirt. His body was pale and waxy, like a fungus. His upper chest was heavy, his belly too. She put her hands to his face. He kissed her fingertips.

"You're beautiful," he said, spitting the words out as though they'd been vexing him for hours.

"Am I?"

"You know you are. Lovely. Loveliest woman I ever set eyes on."

"That's gallant of you," she said, and turned back to the door. Behind her she heard his belt buckle clink, and the sound of cloth slipping over skin as he dropped his trousers.

So far and no farther, she thought. She

had no wish to see him babe-naked. It was enough to have him like this—

She reached into the jacket pocket.

"Oh dear," the lamb suddenly said.

She let the knife lie. "What is it?" she asked, turning to look at him. If the ring on his finger hadn't already given his status away, she would have known him to be a married man by the underpants he wore: baggy and over-washed, an unflattering garment bought by a wife who had long since ceased to think of her husband in sexual terms.

"I think I need to empty my bladder," he said. "Too many whiskies."

She shrugged a small shrug, and turned back to the door.

"Won't be a moment," he said at her back. But her hand was in the jacket pocket before the words were out, and as he stepped towards the door, she turned on him, slaughtering knife in hand.

His pace was too quick to see the blade until the very last moment, and even then it was bemusement that crossed his face, not fear. It was a short-lived look. The knife was in him a moment after, slicing his belly with the ease of a blade in overripe cheese. She opened one cut, and then another.

As the blood started, she was certain the room flickered, the bricks and mortar trembling to see the spurts that flew from him.

She had a breath's length to admire the phenomena, no more, before the lamb let out a wheezing curse, and—instead of moving out of the knife's range as she had anticipated—took a step toward her and knocked the weapon from her hand. It spun across the floorboards and collided with the skirting. Then he was upon her.

He put his hand into her hair and took a fistful. It seemed his intention was not violence but escape, for he relinquished his hold as soon as he'd pulled away from the door. She fell against the wall, looking up to see him wrestling with the door handle, his free hand clamped to his cuts.

She was quick now. Across to where the knife lay, up, and back toward him in one fluid motion. He had got the door open by inches, but not far enough. She brought the knife down in the middle of his pockmarked back. He yelled, and released the door handle. She was already drawing the knife out, and plunging into him a second time, and now a third and a fourth. Indeed she lost count of the wounds she made, her attack lent venom by his refusal to lie down and die. He stumbled around the room, grieving and complaining, blood following blood onto his buttocks and legs. Finally, after an age of this farcical stuff, he keeled over and hit the floor.

This time she was certain her senses did not deceive her. The room, or the spirit in it, responded with soft sighs of anticipation.

Somewhere, a bell was ringing . . .

Almost as an afterthought, she registered that the lamb had stopped breathing. She crossed the blood-spangled floor to where he lay, and said:

"Enough?"

Then she went to wash her face.

As she moved down the landing she heard the room groan—there was no other word for it. She stopped in her tracks, almost tempted to go back. But the blood was drying on her hands, and its stickiness revolted her.

In the bathroom she stripped off her flower-patterned blouse, and rinsed first her hands, then her speckled arms, and finally her neck. The dowsing both chilled and braced her. It felt good. That done, she washed the knife, rinsed the sink and returned along the landing without bothering to dry herself or to dress.

She had no need for either. The room was like a furnace, as the dead man's energies pulsed from his body. They didn't get far. Already the blood on the floor was crawling away toward the wall where Frank was, the beads seeming to boil and evaporate as they came within range of the skirting boards. She watched, entranced. But there was more. Something was happening to the corpse. It was being drained of every nutritious element, the body convulsing as its innards were sucked out, gases moaning in its bowels and throat, the skin dessicating in front of her startled eyes. At one point the plastic teeth dropped back into the gullet, the gums withered around them.

And in mere moments, it was done. Anything the body might have usefully offered by way of nourishment had been taken; the husk that remained would not have sustained a family of fleas. She was impressed.

Suddenly, the bulb began to flicker. She looked to the wall, expecting it to tremble and spit her lover from hiding. But no. The bulb went out. There was only the dim light that crept through the age-beaten blind.

"Where are you?" she said.

The walls remained mute.

"Where are you?"

Still nothing. The room was cooling. Her breasts had grown gooseflesh. She peered down at the luminous watch on the lamb's shriveled arm. It ticked away, indifferent to the apocalypse that had overtaken its owner. It read 4:41. Rory would be back anytime after 5:15, depending on how dense the traffic was. She had work to do before then.

Bundling up the blue suit and the rest of his clothes, she put them in several plastic bags, and then went in search of a larger bag for the remains. She had expected Frank to be here to help her with this labor, but as he hadn't shown she had no choice but to do it herself. When she came back to the room, the deterioration of the lamb was still continuing, though now much slowed. Perhaps Frank was still finding nutriments to squeeze from the corpse, but she doubted it. More likely the pauperized body, sucked clean of marrow and every vital fluid, was no longer strong enough to support itself. When she had parceled it up in the bag, it was the weight of a small child, no more. Sealing the bag up, she was about to take it down to the car when she heard the front door open.

The sound undammed all the panic she'd so assiduously kept from herself. She began to shake. Tears pricked her sinuses.

"Not now . . ." she told herself, but the feelings would simply not be suppressed any longer.

In the hallway below, Rory said: "Sweetheart?"

Sweetheart! She could have laughed, but for the terror. She was here if he wanted to find her—his sweetheart, his honeybun—with her breasts new-washed, and a dead man in her arms.

"Where are you?"

She hesitated before replying, not certain that her larynx was the equal of the deception.

He called a third time, his voice changing timbre as he walked through into the kitchen. It would take him a moment only to discover that she wasn't at the cooker stirring sauce; then he would come back and head up the stairs. She had ten seconds, fifteen at most.

Attempting to keep her tread as light as possible, for fear he heard her movements overhead, she carried the bundle to the spare room at the end of the landing. Too small to be used as a bedroom (except perhaps for a child), they had used it as a dump. Half-emptied tea chests, pieces of furniture they had not found a place for, all manner of rubbish. Here she laid the body to rest awhile, behind an upended armchair. Then she locked the door behind her, just as Rory called from the bottom of the stairs. He was coming up.

"Julia? Julia, sweetheart. Are you there?"

She slipped into the bathroom, and consulted the mirror. It showed her a flushed portrait. She picked up the blouse she'd left hanging over the side of the bath and put it on. It smelled stale, and there was undoubtedly blood spattered between the flowers, but she had nothing else to wear.

He was coming along the landing; she heard his elephantine tread.

"Julia?"

This time, she answered—making no attempt to disguise the tremulous quality of her voice. The mirror had confirmed what she feared: that there was no way she could pass herself off as undistressed. She was obliged to make a virtue of the liability.

"Are you all right?" he asked her. He was outside the door.

"No," she said. "I'm feeling sick."

"Oh, darling . . ."

"I'll be fine in a minute."

He tried the handle, but she'd bolted the door.

"Can you leave me alone for a little while?"

"Do you want a doctor?"

"No," she told him. "No. Really. But I wouldn't mind a brandy—"

"Brandy . . ."

"I'll be down in two ticks."

"Whatever madam wants," he quipped. She counted his steps as he trudged to the stairs, then descended. Once she'd calculated that he was out of earshot, she slid back the bolt and stepped onto the landing.

The late afternoon light was failing quickly; the landing was a murky tunnel.

Downstairs, she heard the clink of glass on glass. She moved as quickly as she dared to Frank's room.

There was no sound from the gloomed interior. The walls no longer trembled, nor did distant bells toll. She pushed the door open; it creaked slightly.

She had not entirely tidied up after her labors. There was dust on the floor, human dust, and fragments of dried flesh. She went down on her haunches and collected them up diligently. Rory had been right. What a perfect hausfrau she made.

As she stood up again, something shifted

in the ever-denser shadows of the room. She looked in the direction of the movement, but before her eyes could make sense of the form in the corner, a voice said: "Don't look at me."

It was a tired voice—the voice of somebody used up by events; but it was *concrete*. The syllables were carried on the same air that she breathed.

"Frank," she said.

"Yes . . ." came the broken voice, "it's me."

From downstairs, Rory called up to her. "Are you feeling better?"

She went to the door.

"Much better," she responded. At her back the hidden thing said: *"Don't let him near me,"* the words coming fast and fierce.

"It's all right," she whispered to him. Then, to Rory: "I'll be with you in a minute. Put on some music. Something soothing."

Rory replied that he would, and retired to the lounge.

"I'm only half-made," Frank's voice said. "I don't want you to see me . . . don't want *anybody* to see me . . . not like this . . ." The words were halting once more, and wretched. "I have to have more blood, Julia."

"More?"

"And soon."

"How much more?" she asked the shadows. This time she caught a better glimpse of what lay in wait there. No wonder he wanted no one to look.

"Just *more,*" he said. Though the volume was barely above a whisper, there was an urgency in the voice that made her afraid.

"I have to go . . ." she said, hearing music from below.

This time the darkness made no reply. At the door, she turned back.

"I'm glad you came," she said. As she closed the door, she heard a sound not unlike laughter behind her, nor unlike sobs.

SEVEN

"*K*irsty? Is that you?"
"Yes? Who is this?"
"It's Rory . . ."

The line was watery, as though the deluge outside had seeped down the phone. Still, she was happy to hear from him. He called up so seldom, and when he did it was usually on behalf of both himself and Julia. Not this time however. This time Julia was the subject under discussion.

"There's something wrong with her, Kirsty," he said. "I don't know what."

"Ill, you mean?"

"Maybe. She's just so strange with me. And she looks terrible."

"Have you said anything to her?"

"She says she's fine. But she isn't. I wondered if maybe she'd spoken with you."

"I haven't set eyes on her since your housewarming."

"That's another thing. She doesn't even want to leave the house. That's not like her."

"Do you want me to . . . to have a word with her?"

"Would you?"

"I don't know if it'll do any good, but I'll try."

"Don't say anything about me talking to you."

"Of course not. I'll call in at the house tomorrow—"

("Tomorrow. It has to be tomorrow."

"Yes . . . I know."

"I'm afraid I'll lose my grip, Julia. Start slipping back.")

"I'll give you a call from the office on Thursday. You can tell me what you make of her."

("Slipping back?"
"They'll know I've gone by now."
"Who will?"
"The Gash. The bastards that took me . . ."
"They're waiting for you?"
"Just beyond the wall.")

Rory told her how grateful he was, and she in turn told him that it was the least a friend could do. Then he put down the phone, leaving her listening to the rain on the empty line.

Now they were both Julia's creatures, looking after her welfare, fretting for her if she had bad dreams.

No matter, it was a kind of togetherness.

2

The man with the white tie had not bided his time. Almost as soon as he set eyes on Julia he came across to her. She decided, even as he approached, that he was not suitable. Too big; too confident. After the way the first one had fought, she was determined to choose with care. So, when White Tie asked what she was drinking, she told him to leave her be.

He was apparently used to rejections, and

took it in his stride, withdrawing to the bar.
She returned to her drink.

It was raining heavily today—had been
raining now for seventy-two hours, on and
off—and there were fewer customers than
there had been the week before. One or two
drowned rats headed in from the street, but
none looked her way for more than a few moments. And time was moving on. It was already
past two. She wasn't going to risk getting
caught again by Rory's return. She emptied her
glass, and decided that this was not Frank's
lucky day. Then she stepped out of the bar into
the downpour, put up her umbrella, and
headed back to the car. As she went she heard
footsteps behind her, and then White Tie was
at her side and saying: "My hotel's nearby."

"Oh . . ." she said and kept on walking.
But he wasn't going to be shrugged off so easily.

"I'm only here for two days," he said.

Don't tempt me, she thought.

"Just looking for some companionship
. . ." he went on. "I haven't spoken to a soul."

"Is that right?"

He took hold of her wrist. A grip so tight
she almost cried out. That was when she knew
she was going to have to kill him. He seemed
to see the desire in her eyes.

"My hotel?" he said.

"I don't much like hotels. They're so impersonal."

"Have you got a better idea?" he said to her.

She had, of course.

He hung his dripping raincoat on the hall stand, and she offered him a drink, which he welcomed. His name was Patrick, and he was from Newcastle.

"Down on business. Can't seem to get much done."

"Why's that?"

He shrugged. "I'm probably a bad salesman. Simple as that."

"What do you sell?" she asked him.

"What do you care?" he replied, razor quick.

She grinned. She would have to get him upstairs quickly, before she started to enjoy his company.

"Why don't we dispense with the small talk?" she said. It was a stale line, but it was the first thing that came to her tongue. He swallowed the last of his drink in one gulp, and went where she led.

This time she had not left the door ajar. It was locked, which plainly intrigued him.

"After you," he said, when the door swung open.

She went first. He followed. This time, she had decided, there would be no stripping. If some nourishment was soaked up by his clothes then so be it; she was not going to give him a chance to realize that they weren't alone in the room.

"Going to fuck on the floor, are we?" he asked casually.

"Any objections?"

"Not if it suits you," he said and clamped his mouth over hers, his tongue frisking her teeth for cavities. There was some passion in him, she mused; she could feel him hard against her already. But she had work to do here: blood to spill and a mouth to feed.

She broke his kiss, and tried to slip from his arms. The knife was back in the jacket on the door. While it was out of reach she had little power to resist him.

"What's the problem?" he said.

"No problem . . ." she murmured. "There's no hurry either. We've got all the time in the world." She touched the front of his trousers, to reassure him. Like a stroked dog, he closed his eyes.

"You're a strange one," he said.

"Don't look," she told him.

"Huh?"

"Keep your eyes closed."

He frowned, but obeyed. She took a step backward toward the door, and half turned to fumble in the depths of the pocket, glancing back to see that he was still blind.

He was, and unzipping himself. As her hand clasped the knife, the shadows growled.

He heard the noise. His eyes sprang open.

"What was that?" he said, reeling round and peering into the darkness.

"It was nothing," she insisted, as she pulled the knife from its hiding place. He was moving away from her, across the room.

"There's somebody—"

"*Don't.*"

"—here."

The last syllable faltered on his lips, as he glimpsed a fretful motion in the corner beside the window.

"What . . . in God's . . .?" he began. As he pointed into the darkness she was at him, and slicing his neck open with a butcher's efficiency. Blood jumped immediately, a fat spurt that hit the wall with a wet thud. She heard Frank's pleasure, and then the dying man's complaint, long and low. His hand went up to his neck to stem the pulse, but she was at him again, slicing his pleading hand, his face. He staggered, he sobbed. Finally, he collapsed, twitching.

She stepped away from him to avoid the flailing legs. In the corner of the room she saw Frank rocking to and fro.

"Good woman . . ." he said.

Was it her imagination, or was his voice already stronger than it had been, more like the voice she'd heard in her head a thousand times these plundered years?

The door bell rang. She froze.

"Oh Jesus," her mouth said.

"It's all right . . ." the shadow replied. "He's as good as dead."

She looked at the man in the white tie and saw that Frank was right. The twitching had all but ceased.

"He's big," said Frank. "And healthy."

He was moving into her sight, too greedy for sustenance to prohibit her stare; she saw him plainly now for the first time. He was a travesty. Not just of humanity, of life. She looked away.

The door bell was ringing again, and for longer.

"Go and answer it," Frank told her.

She made no reply.

"Go on," he told her, turning his foul head in her direction, his eyes keen and bright in the surrounding corruption.

The bell rang a third time.

"Your caller is very insistent," he said, trying persuasion where demands had failed. "I really think you should answer the door."

She backed away from him, and he turned his attentions back to the body on the floor.

Again, the bell.

It was better to answer it perhaps (she was already out of the room, trying not to hear the sounds Frank was making), better to open the door to the day. It would be a man selling insurance, most likely, or a Jehovah's Witness, with news of salvation. Yes, she wouldn't mind hearing that. The bell rang again. "Coming," she said, hurrying now for fear he leave. She had welcome on her face when she opened the door. It died immediately.

"Kirsty."

"I was just about to give up on you."

"I was . . . I was asleep."

"Oh."

Kirsty looked at the apparition that had opened the door to her. From Rory's description she'd expected a washed-out creature.

What she saw was quite the reverse. Julia's face was flushed: strands of sweat-darkened hair glued to her brow. She did not look like a woman who had just risen from sleep. A bed, perhaps, but not sleep.

"I just called by"—Kirsty said—"for a chat."

Julia made a half shrug.

"Well, it's not convenient just at the moment," she said.

"I see."

"Maybe we could speak later in the week?"

Kirsty's gaze drifted past Julia to the coat stand in the hall. A man's gabardine hung from one of the pegs, still damp.

"Is Rory in?" she ventured.

"No," Julia said. "Of course not. He's at work." Her face hardened. "Is that what you came round for?" she said. "To see Rory?"

"No, I—"

"You don't have to ask my permission, you know. He's a grown man. You two can do what the fuck you like."

Kirsty didn't try to debate the point. The volte-face left her dizzied.

"Go home," Julia said. "I don't want to talk to you."

She slammed the door.

Kirsty stood on the step for half a minute, shaking. She had little doubt of what was going on. The dripping raincoat, Julia's agitation— her flushed face, her sudden anger. She had a lover in the house. Poor Rory had misread all the signs.

She deserted the doorstep and started down the path to the street. A crowd of thoughts jostled for her attention. At last, one came clear of the pack: How would she tell Rory? His heart would break, she had no doubt of that. And she, the luckless tale-teller, she would be tainted with the news, wouldn't she? She felt tears close.

They didn't come, however; another sensation, more insistent, overtook as she stepped onto the pavement from the path.

She was being watched. She could feel the look at the back of her head. Was it Julia? Somehow, she thought not. The lover then. Yes, the lover!

Safely out of the shadow of the house, she succumbed to the urge to turn and look.

In the damp room, Frank stared through the hole he had made in the blind. The visitor—whose face he vaguely recognized—was staring up at the house, at his very window, indeed. Confident that she could see nothing of him, he stared back. He had certainly set his eyes on more voluptuous creatures, but something about her lack of glamour engaged him. Such women were in his experience often more entertaining company than beauties like Julia. They could be flattered or bullied into acts the beauties would never countenance and be grateful for the attention. Perhaps she would come back, this woman. He hoped she would.

Kirsty scanned the facade of the house, but it was blank; the windows were either empty or curtained. Yet the feeling of being watched persisted; indeed it was so strong she turned away in embarrassment.

The rain started again as she walked along Lodovico Street, and she welcomed it. It cooled her blushes, and gave cover to tears that would be postponed no longer.

------------------ 3 ------------------

Julia had gone back upstairs trembling, and found White Tie at the door. Or rather, his head. This time, either out of an excess of greed or malice, Frank had dismembered the corpse. Pieces of bones and dried meat lay scattered about the room.

There was no sign of the gourmet himself.

She turned back toward the door, and he was there, blocking her path. Mere minutes had passed since she'd seen him bending to drain energy from the dead man. In that brief time he had changed out of all recognition. Where there had been withered cartilage, there was not ripening muscle; the map of his arteries and veins was being drawn anew: they pulsed with stolen life. There was even a sprouting of hair, somewhat premature perhaps given his absence of skin, on the raw ball of his head.

None of this sweetened his appearance a jot. Indeed in many ways it worsened it. Previously there had been scarcely anything recognizable about him, but now there were scraps of humanity everywhere, throwing into yet greater relief the catastrophic nature of his wounding.

There was worse to come. He spoke, and when he spoke it was with a voice that was indisputably Frank's. The broken syllables had gone.

"I feel pain," he said.

His browless, half-lidded eyes were watching her every response. She tried to conceal the queasiness she felt, but knew the disguise inadequate.

"My nerves are working again," he was telling her, "and they *hurt.*"

"What can I do about it?" she asked him.

"Maybe . . . maybe some bandages."

"Bandages?"

"Help me bind myself together."

"If that's what you want."

"But I need more than that, Julia. I need another body."

"Another?" she said. Was there no end to this?

"What's to lose?" he replied, moving closer to her. At his sudden proximity she became very anxious. Reading the fear in her face, he stopped his advance.

"I'll be whole soon . . ." he promised her, "and when I am . . ."

"I'd better clear up," she said, averting her gaze from him.

"When I am, sweet Julia . . ."

"Rory will be home soon."

"*Rory!*" He spat the name out. "My darling brother! How in God's name did you come to marry such a dullard?"

She felt a spasm of anger toward Frank. "I

loved him," she said. And then, after a moment's pondering, corrected herself. "I thought I loved him."

His laugh only made his dreadful nakedness more apparent. "How can you have believed that?" he said. "He's a slug. Always was. Always will be. Never had any sense of adventure."

"Unlike you."

"Unlike me."

She looked down at the floor; a dead man's hand lay between them. For an instant she was almost overwhelmed by self-revulsion. All that she had done, and dreamed of doing, in the last few days rose up in front of her: a parade of seductions that had ended in death— all for this death that she had hoped so fervently would end in seduction. She was as damned as he, she thought; no fouler ambition could nest in his head than presently cooed and fluttered in hers.

Well . . . it was done.

"Heal me," he whispered to her. The harshness had gone from his voice. He spoke like a lover. "Heal me . . . please."

"I will," she said. "I promise you I will."

"And then we'll be together."

She frowned.

"What about Rory?"

"We're brothers, under the skin," Frank said. "I'll make him see the wisdom of this, the miracle of it. You don't belong to him Julia. Not anymore."

"No," she said. It was true.

"We belong to each other. That's what you want isn't it?"

"It's what I want."

"You know I think if I'd had you I wouldn't have despaired," he said to her. "Wouldn't have given away my body and soul so cheaply."

"Cheaply?"

"For pleasure. For mere sensuality. In you . . ." here he moved toward her again. This time his words held her; she didn't retreat. "In you I might have discovered some reason to live."

"I'm here," she said. Without thinking, she reached across and touched him. The body was hot, and damp. His pulse seemed to be everywhere. In every tender bud of nerve, in each burgeoning sinew. The contact excited her. It was as if, until this moment, she had never quite believed him to be real. Now it was incontestable. She had *made* this man, or remade him, used her wit and her cunning to give him substance. The thrill she felt, touching this too vulnerable body, was the thrill of ownership.

"This is the most dangerous time," he told her. "Before now, I could hide myself. I was practically nothing at all. But not anymore."

"No. I've thought of that."

"We must be done with it quickly. I must be strong and whole, at whatever cost. You agree?"

"Of course."

"After that there'll be an end to the waiting, Julia."

The pulse in him seemed to quicken at the thought.

Then he was kneeling in front of her. His unfinished hands were at her hips, then his mouth.

Forsaking the dregs of her distaste, she put her hand upon his head, and felt the hair— silken, like a baby's—and the shell of his skull beneath. He had learned nothing of delicacy since last he'd held her. But despair had taught her the fine art of squeezing blood from stones; with time she would have love from this hateful thing, or know the reason why.

EIGHT

1

There was thunder that night. A storm without rain, which made the air smell of steel.

Kirsty had never slept well. Even as a child, though her mother had known lullabies enough to pacify nations, the girl had never found slumber easy. It wasn't that she had bad dreams; or at least none that lingered until morning. It was that sleep itself—the act of closing the eyes and relinquishing control of her consciousness—was something she was temperamentally unsuited to.

Tonight, with the thunder so loud and the lightning so bright, she was happy. She had an excuse to forsake her tangled bed, and drink tea, and watch the spectacle from her window.

It gave her time to think, as well—time to turn over the problem that had vexed her since leaving the house on Lodovico Street. But she was still no nearer an answer.

One particular doubt nagged. Suppose she was wrong about what she'd seen? Suppose she'd misconstrued the evidence, and Julia had a perfectly good explanation? She would lose Rory at a stroke.

And yet, how could she remain silent? She couldn't bear to think of the woman laughing behind his back, exploiting his gentility, his naïveté. The thought made her blood boil.

The only other option was to wait and watch, to see if she could gain some incontrovertible evidence. If her worst suppositions were then confirmed, she would have no choice but to tell Rory all she'd seen.

Yes. That was the answer. Wait and watch, watch and wait.

The thunder rolled around for long hours, denying her sleep until nearly four. When, fi-

nally, she did sleep, it was the slumber of a
watcher and waiter. Light, and full of sighs.

—————————— 2 ——————————

The storm made a ghost train of the
house. Julia sat downstairs, and counted the
beats between the flash and the fury that came
on its heels. She had never liked thunder. She,
a murderess; she, a consorter with the living
dead. It was another paradox to add to the
thousand she'd found at work in herself of late.
She thought more than once of going upstairs,
and taking some comfort with the prodigy, but
knew that it would be unwise. Rory might return at any moment from his office party. He
would be drunk, on past experience, and full of
unwelcome fondness.

The storm crept closer. She put on the
television, to block out the din, which it
scarcely did.

At eleven. Rory came home, wreathed in
smiles. He had good news. In the middle of the
party his supervisor had taken him aside, com-
mended him for his excellent work, and spoken
of great things for the future. Julia listened to
his retelling of the exchange, hoping that his

inebriation would blind him to her indifference. At last, his news told, he threw off his
jacket and sat down on the sofa beside her.

"Poor you," he said. "You don't like the
thunder."

"I'm fine," she said.

"Are you sure?"

"Yes. Fine."

He leaned across to her and nuzzled her
ear.

"You're sweaty," she said matter-of-
factly. He didn't cease his overtures, however,
unwilling to lower his baton now that he'd
begun.

"Please, Rory—" she said. "I don't want
this."

"Why not? What did I do?"

"Nothing," she said, pretending some interest in the television. "You're fine."

"Oh, is that right?" he said. *"You're* fine.
I'm fine. Everybody's fucking fine."

She stared at the flickering screen. The
late evening news had just begun, the usual cup
of sorrows full to brimming. Rory talked on,
drowning out the newscaster's voice with his
diatribe. She didn't much mind. What did the
world have to tell her? Little enough. Whereas
she, *she* had news for the world that it would

reel to hear. About the condition of the damned; about love lost, and then found; about what despair and desire have in common.

"Please, Julia"—Rory was saying—"just speak to me."

The pleas demanded her attention. He looked, she thought, like the boy in the photographs—his body hirsute and bloated, his clothes those of an adult—but still, in essence, a boy, with his bewildered gaze and sulky mouth. She remembered Frank's question: *"How could you ever have married such a dullard?"* Thinking of it, a sour smile creased her lips. He looked at her, his puzzlement deepening.

"What's so funny, damn you?"

"Nothing."

He shook his head, dull anger replacing the sulk. A peal of thunder followed the lightning with barely a beat intervening. As it came, there was a noise from the floor above. She turned her attention back to the television, to divert Rory's interest. But it was a vain attempt; he'd heard the sound.

"What the fuck was that?"

"Thunder."

He stood up. "No," he said. "Something else." He was already at the door.

A dozen options raced through her head, none of them practical. He wrestled drunkenly with the door handle.

"Maybe I left a window open," she said and got up. "I'll go and see."

"I can do it," he replied. "I'm not totally inept."

"Nobody said—" she began, but he wasn't listening. As he stepped out into the hallway the lightning came with the thunder: loud and bright. As she went in pursuit of him another flash came fast upon the first, accompanied by a bowel-rocking crash. Rory was already halfway up the stairs.

"It was nothing!" she shouted after him. He made no reply but climbed on to the top of the stairs. She followed.

"Don't . . ." she said to him, in a lull between one peal and the next. He heard her this time. Or rather, chose to listen. When she reached the top of the stairs he was waiting.

"Something wrong?" he said.

She hid her trepidation behind a shrug. "You're being silly," she replied softly.

"Am I?"

"It was just the thunder."

His face, lit from the hall below, suddenly

softened. "Why do you treat me like shit?" he asked her.

"You're just tired," she told him.

"Why though?" he persisted, childlike. "What have I ever done to you?"

"It's all right," she said. "Really, Rory. Everything's all right." The same hypnotic banalities, over and over.

Again, the thunder. And beneath the din, another sound. She cursed Frank's indiscretion.

Rory turned, and looked along the darkened landing.

"Hear that?" he said.

"No."

His limbs dogged by drink, he moved away from her. She watched him recede into shadow. Lightning, spilling through the open bedroom door, flash—lit him; then darkness again. He was walking toward the damp room. Toward Frank.

"Wait . . ." she said, and went after him.

He didn't halt, but covered the few yards to the door. As she reached him, his hand was closing on the handle.

Inspired by panic, she reached out and touched his cheek. "I'm afraid . . ." she said.

He looked round at her woozily.

"What of?" he asked her.

She moved her hand to his lips, letting him taste the fear on her fingers.

"The storm," she said.

She could see the wetness of his eyes in the gloom, little more. Was he swallowing the hook, or spitting it out?

Then: "Poor baby," he said.

Swallowed, she elated, and reaching down she put her hand over his and drew it from the door. If Frank so much as breathed now, all was lost.

"Poor baby," he said again and wrapped an embrace around her. His balance was not too good; he was a lead weight in her arms.

"Come on," she said, coaxing him away from the door. He went with her for a couple of stumbling paces, and then lost his equilibrium. She let go of him, and reached out to the wall for support. The lightning came again, and by it she saw that his eyes had found her, and glittered.

"I love you," he said, stepping across the hallway to where she stood. He pressed against her, so heavily there was no resisting. His head went to the crook of her neck, muttering sweet talk into her skin. Now he was kissing her. She wanted to throw him off. More, she wanted to take him by his clammy hand and show him the death-defying monster he had been so close to stumbling across.

But Frank wasn't ready for that confrontation, not yet. All she could do was endure Rory's caresses and hope that exhaustion claimed him quickly.

"Why don't we go downstairs?" she suggested.

He muttered something into her neck and didn't move. His left hand was on her breast, the other clasped around her waist. She let him work his fingers beneath her blouse. To resist at this juncture would only inflame him afresh.

"I need you," he said, raising his mouth to her ear. Once, half a lifetime ago, her heart had seemed to skip at such a profession. Now she knew better. Her heart was no acrobat; there was no tingle in the coils of her abdomen. Only the steady workings of her body. Breath drawn, blood circulated, food pulped and purged. Thinking of her anatomy thus, untainted by romanticism—as a collection of natural imperatives housed in muscle and bone—she found it easier to let him strip her blouse and put his face to her breasts. Her nerve endings dutifully responded to his tongue, but again, it was merely an anatomy lesson. She stood back in the dome of her skull, and was unmoved.

He was unbuttoning himself now; she caught sight of the boastful plum as he stroked it against her thigh. Now he opened her legs, and pulled her underwear down just far enough to give him access. She made no objection, nor even a sound, as he made his entrance.

His own din began almost immediately, feeble claims to love and lust hopelessly tangled together. She half listened, and let him work at his play, his face buried in her hair.

Closing her eyes, she tried to picture better times, but the lightning spoiled her dreaming. As sound followed light, she opened her eyes again to see that the door of the damp room had been opened two or three inches. In the narrow gap between door and frame she could just make out a glistening figure, watching them.

She could not see Frank's eyes, but she felt them sharpened beyond pricking by envy and rage. Nor did she look away, but stared on at the shadow while Rory's moans increased. And at the end one moment became another, and she was lying on the bed with her wedding dress crushed beneath her, while a black and

scarlet beast crept up between her legs to give
her a sample of its love.

"Poor baby," was the last thing Rory said
as sleep overcame him. He lay on the bed still
dressed; she made no attempt to strip him.
When his snores were even, she left him to it,
and went back to the room.

Frank was standing beside the window,
watching the storm move to the southeast. He
had torn the blind away. Lamplight washed the
walls.

"He heard you," she said.

"I had to see the storm," he replied simply. "I needed it."

"He almost found you, damn it."

Frank shook his head. "There's no such
thing as almost," he said, still staring out of the
window. Then, after a pause: "I want to be out
there. I want to *have* it all again."

"I know."

"No you don't," he told her. "You've no
conception of the hunger I've got on me."

"Tomorrow then," she said. "I'll get another body tomorrow."

"Yes. You do that. And I want some other
stuff. A radio, for one. I want to know what's

going on out there. And food: proper food.
Fresh bread—"

"Whatever you need."

"—and ginger. The preserved kind, you
know? In syrup."

"I know."

He glanced round at her briefly, but he
wasn't seeing her. There was too much world
to be reacquainted with tonight.

"I didn't realize it was autumn," he said,
and went back to watching the storm.

NINE

The first thing Kirsty noticed when she came round the corner of Lodovico Street the following day was that the blind had gone from the upper front window. Sheets of newspaper had been taped against the glass in its place.

She found herself a vantage point in the shelter of a holly hedge, from which she hoped she could watch the house but remain unseen. Then she settled down for her vigil.

It was not quickly rewarded. Two hours and more went by before she saw Julia leave the house, another hour and a quarter before she returned, by which time Kirsty's feet were numb with cold.

Julia had not returned alone. The man she was with was not known to Kirsty, nor indeed did he look to be a likely member of Julia's circle. From a distance he appeared to be in middle age, stocky, balding. When he followed Julia into the house he gave a nervous backward glance, as if fearful of voyeurs.

She waited in her hiding place for a further quarter of an hour, not certain of what to do next. Did she linger here until the man emerged, and challenge him? Or did she go to the house and try to talk her way inside? Neither option was particularly attractive. She decided not to decide. Instead she would get closer to the house, and see what inspiration the moment brought.

The answer was, very little. As she made her way up the path her feet itched to turn and carry her away. Indeed she was within an ace of doing just that when she heard a shout from within.

The man's name was Sykes, Stanley Sykes. Nor was that all he'd told Julia on the way back from the bar. She knew his wife's name (Maudie) and occupation (assistant chiropodist); she'd had pictures of the children (Rebecca and Ethan) provided for her to coo over. The man seemed to be defying her to continue the seduction. She merely smiled, and told him he was a lucky man.

But once in the house, things had begun to go awry. Halfway up the stairs friend Sykes had suddenly announced that what they were doing was *wrong*—that God saw them, and knew their hearts, and found them wanting. She had done her best to calm him, but he was not to be won back from the Lord. Instead, he lost his temper and flailed out at her. He might have done worse, in his righteous wrath, but for the voice that had called him from the landing. He'd stopped hitting her instantly and become so pale it was as if he believed God himself was doing the calling. Then Frank had appeared at the top of the stairs, in all his glory. Sykes had loosed a cry, and tried to run. But Julia was quick. She had her hand on him long enough for Frank to descend the few stairs and make a permanent arrest.

She had not realized, until she heard the creak and snap of bone as Frank took hold of his prey, how strong he had become of late:

stronger surely than a natural man. At Frank's touch Sykes had shouted again. To silence him, Frank wrenched off his jaw.

The second shout that Kirsty had heard had ended abruptly, but she read enough panic in the din to have her at the door and on the verge of knocking.

Only then did she think better of it. Instead, she slipped down the side of the house, doubting with every step the wisdom of this, but equally certain that a frontal assault would get her nowhere. The gate that offered access to the back garden was lacking a bolt. She slipped through, her ears alive to every sound, especially that of her own feet. From the house, nothing. Not so much as a moan.

Leaving the gate open in case she should need a quick retreat, she hurried to the back door. It was unlocked. This time, she let doubt slow her step. Maybe she should go and call Rory, bring him to the house. But by that time whatever was happening inside would be over, and she knew damn well that unless Julia was caught red-handed she would slide from under any accusation. No, this was the only way. She stepped inside.

The house remained completely quiet. There was not even a footfall to help her locate the actors she'd come to view. She moved to the kitchen door, and from there through to the dining room. Her stomach twitched; her throat was suddenly so dry she could barely swallow.

From dining room to lounge, and thence into the hallway. Still nothing, no whisper or sigh. Julia and her companion could only be upstairs, which suggested that she had been wrong, thinking she heard fear in the shouts. Perhaps it was pleasure that she'd heard. An orgasmic whoop, instead of the terror she'd taken it for. It was an easy mistake to make.

The front door was on her right, mere yards away. She could still slip out and away, the coward in her tempted, and no one be any the wiser. But a fierce curiosity had seized her, a desire to know (to *see*) the mysteries the house held, and be done with them. As she climbed the stairs the curiosity mounted to a kind of exhilaration.

She reached the top, and began to make her way along the landing. The thought occurred now that the birds had flown, that while she had been creeping through from the back of the house they had left via the front.

The first door on the left was the bedroom: if they were mating anywhere, Julia and her paramour, it would surely be here. But no. The door stood ajar; she peered in. The bed-spread was uncreased.

Then, a misshapen cry. So near, so loud, her heart missed its rhythm.

She ducked out of the bedroom, to see a figure lurch from one of the rooms farther along the landing. It took her a moment to recognize the fretful man who had arrived with Julia—and only then by his clothes. The rest was changed, horribly changed. A wasting dis-ease had seized him in the minutes since she'd seen him on the step, shriveling his flesh on the bone.

Seeing Kirsty, he threw himself toward her, seeking what fragile protection she could offer. He had got no more than a pace from the door however, when a form spilled into sight behind him. It too seemed diseased, its body bandaged from head to foot—the bindings stained by issues of blood and pus. There was nothing in its speed, however, or the ferocity of its subsequent attack, that suggested sickness. Quite the reverse. It reached for the fleeing man and took hold of him by the neck. Kirsty let out a cry, as the captor drew its prey back into its embrace.

The victim made what little complaint his

dislocated face was capable of. Then the antag-
onist tightened its embrace. The body trembled and twitched; its legs buckled. Blood
spurted from eyes and nose and mouth. Spots
of it filled the air like hot hail, breaking against
her brow. The sensation snapped her from her
inertia. This was no time to wait and watch.
She *ran*.

The monster made no pursuit. She
reached the top of the stairs without being
overtaken. But as her foot descended, it addressed her.

Its voice was . . . familiar.

"There you are," it said.

It spoke with melting tones, as if it knew
her. She stopped.

"Kirsty," it said. "Wait a while."

Her head told her to run. Her gut defied
the wisdom, however. It wanted to remember
whose voice this was, speaking from the binding. She could still make good her escape, she
reasoned; she had an eight-yard start. She
looked round at the figure. The body in its arms
had curled up, fetally, legs against chest. The
beast dropped it.

"You killed him . . ." she said.

The thing nodded. It had no apologies to
make, apparently, to either victim or witness.

"We'll mourn him later," it told her and took a step toward her.

"Where's Julia?" Kirsty demanded.

"Don't you fret. All's well . . ." the voice said. She was so close to remembering who it was.

As she puzzled it took another step, one hand upon the wall, as if its balance was still uncertain.

"I saw you," it went on. "And I think you saw me. At the window . . ."

Her mystification increased. Had this thing been in the house that long? If so, surely Rory must—

And then she knew the voice.

"Yes. You do remember. I can see you remember . . ."

It was *Rory's* voice, or rather, a close approximation of it. More guttural, more self-regarding, but the resemblance was uncanny enough to keep her rooted to the spot while the beast shambled within snatching distance of her.

At the last she recanted her fascination, and turned to flee, but the cause was already lost. She heard its step a pace behind her, then felt its fingers at her neck. A cry came to her lips, but it was barely mounted before the thing

had its corrugated palm across her face, cancel-
ing both the shout and the breath it came
upon.

It plucked her up, and took her back the
way she'd come. In vain she struggled against
its hold; the small wounds her fingers made
upon its body—tearing at the bandages and
digging into the rawness beneath—left it entirely unmoved, it seemed. For a horrid moment her heels snagged the corpse on the floor.
Then she was being hauled into the room from
which the living and the dead had emerged. It
smelled of soured milk and fresh meat. When
she was flung down the boards beneath her
were wet and warm.

Her belly wanted to turn inside out. She
didn't fight the instinct, but retched up all that
her stomach held. In the confusion of present
discomfort and anticipated terror she was not
certain of what happened next. Did she
glimpse somebody else (Julia) on the landing as
the door was slammed, or was it shadow? One
way or another it was too late for appeals. She
was alone with the nightmare.

Wiping the bile from her mouth she got
to her feet. Daylight pierced the newspaper at
the window here and there, dappling the room

like sunlight through branches. And through this pastoral, the thing came sniffing her.

"Come to Daddy," it said.

In her twenty-six years she had never heard an easier invitation to refuse.

"Don't touch me," she told it.

It cocked its head a little, as if charmed by this show of propriety. Then it closed in on her, all pus and laughter, and—God help her—*desire*.

She backed a few desperate inches into the corner, until there was nowhere else for her to go.

"Don't you remember me?" it said.

She shook her head.

"Frank," came the reply. "This is brother Frank . . ."

She had met Frank only once, at Alexandra Road. He'd come visiting one afternoon, just before the wedding, more she couldn't recall. Except that she'd hated him on sight.

"Leave me alone," she said as it reached for her. There was a vile finesse in the way his stained fingers touched her breast.

"Don't," she shrieked, "or so help me—"

"What?" said Rory's voice. "What will you do?"

Nothing, was the answer of course. She

was helpless, as only she had ever been in dreams, those dreams of pursuit and assault that her psyche had always staged on a ghetto street in some eternal night. Never—not even in her most witless fantasies—had she antici- pated that the arena would be a room she had walked past a dozen times, in a house where she had been happy, while outside the day went on as ever, gray on gray.

In a futile gesture of disgust, she pushed the investigating hand away.

"Don't be cruel," the thing said, and his fingers found her skin again, as unshooable as October wasps. "What's to be frightened of?"

"Outside . . ." she began, thinking of the horror on the landing.

"A man has to eat," Frank replied. "Surely you can forgive me that?"

Why did she even feel his touch, she won- dered? Why didn't her nerves share her disgust and die beneath his caress?

"This isn't happening," she told herself aloud, but the beast only laughed.

"I used to tell myself that," he said. "Day in, day out. Used to try and dream the agonies away. But you can't. Take it from me. You can't. They have to be endured."

She knew he was telling the truth, the

kind of unsavory truth that only monsters were at liberty to tell. He had no need to flatter or cajole; he had no philosophy to debate, or sermon to deliver. His awful nakedness was a kind of sophistication. Past the lies of faith, and into purer realms.

She knew too that she would *not* endure. That when her pleadings faltered, and Frank claimed her for whatever vileness he had in mind, she would loose such a scream that she would shatter.

Her very sanity was at stake here; she had no choice but to fight back, and quickly.

Before Frank had a chance to press his suit any harder, her hands went up to his face, fingers gouging at his eye holes and mouth. The flesh beneath the bandage had the consistency of jelly; it came away in globs, and with it, a wet heat.

The beast shouted out, his grip on her relaxing. Seizing the moment, she threw herself out from under him, the momentum carrying her against the wall with enough force to badly wind her.

Again, Frank roared. She didn't waste time enjoying his discomfort, but slid along the wall—not trusting her legs sufficiently to move into open territory—toward the door. As she advanced, her feet sent an unlidded jar of preserved ginger rolling across the room, spilling syrup and fruit alike.

Frank turned toward her, the bandaging about his face hanging in scarlet loops where she'd torn it away. In several places the bone was exposed. Even now, he ran his hands over the wounds, roars of horror coming as he sought to measure the degree of his maiming. Had she blinded him? She wasn't sure. Even if she had it was only a matter of time before he located her in this small room, and when he did his rage would know no bounds. She had to reach the door before he reoriented himself.

Faint hope! She hadn't a moment to take a step before he dropped his hands from his face and scanned the room. He saw her, no doubt of that. A beat later, he was bearing down upon her with renewed violence.

At her feet lay a litter of domestic items. The heaviest item amongst them was a plain box. She reached down and picked it up. As she stood upright, he was upon her. She loosed a cry of defiance and swung the box-bearing fist at his head. It connected heavily; bone splintered. The beast tottered backward, and she launched herself toward the door, but before she reached it the shadow swamped her once more, and she was flung backward across the room. It came in a raging pursuit.

This time he had no intention beyond the murderous. His lashes were intended to kill; that they did not was testament less to her speed than to the imprecision of his fury. Nevertheless, one out of every three blows caught her. Gashes opened in her face and upper chest; it was all she could do to prevent herself from fainting.

As she sank beneath his assault, again she remembered the weapon she'd found. The box was still in her hand. She raised it to deliver another blow, but as Frank's eyes came to rest on the box his assault abruptly ceased.

There was a panting respite, in which Kirsty had a chance to wonder if death might not be easier than further flight. Then Frank raised his arm toward her, unfurled his fist and said: "Give it to me."

He wanted his keepsake, it seemed. But she had no intention of relinquishing her only weapon.

"No," she said.

He made the demand a second time, and there was a distinct anxiety in his tone. It seemed the box was too precious for him to risk taking it by force.

"One last time," he said to her. "Then I'll kill you. Give me the box."

She weighed the chances. What had she left to lose?

"Say please," she said.

He regarded her quizzically, a soft growl in his throat. Then, polite as a calculating child, he said, "Please."

The word was her cue. She threw the box at the window with all the strength her trembling arm possessed. It sailed past Frank's head, shattering the glass, and disappeared from sight.

"No!" he shrieked, and was at the window in a heartbeat. *"No! No! No!"*

She raced to the door, her legs threatening to fail her with every step. Then she was out onto the landing. The stairs almost defeated her, but she clung to the bannister like a geriatric, and made it to the hallway without falling.

Above, there was further din. He was calling after her again. But this time she would not be caught. She fled along the hallway to the front door, and flung it open.

The day had brightened since she'd first entered the house—a defiant burst of sunlight before evening fell. Squinting against the glare she started down the pathway. There was glass underfoot, and amongst the shards, her weapon. She picked it up, a souvenir of her defiance, and ran. As she reached the street proper, words began to come—a hopeless babble, fragments of things seen and felt. But Lodovico Street was deserted, so she began to run, and kept running until she had put a good distance between her and the bandaged beast.

Eventually, wandering on some street she didn't recognize, somebody asked her if she needed help. The little kindness defeated her, for the effort of making some coherent reply to the inquiry was too much, and her exhausted mind lost its hold on the light.

TEN

She woke in a blizzard, or such was her first impression. Above her, a perfect whiteness, snow on snow. She was tucked up in snow, pillowed in snow. The blankness was sickening. It seemed to fill up her throat and eyes.

She raised her hands in front of her face; they smelled of an unfamiliar soap, whose perfume was harsh. Now she began to focus: the walls, the pristine sheets, the medication beside the bed. A hospital.

She called out for help. Hours or minutes later, she wasn't sure which, it came, in the form of a nurse who simply said, "You're awake," and went to fetch her superiors.

She told them nothing when they came. She had decided in the time between the nurse's disappearance and reappearance with the doctors that this was not a story she was ready to tell. Tomorrow (maybe) she might find the words to convince them of what she'd seen. But today? If she tried to explain, they would stroke her brow and tell her to hush her nonsense, condescend to her and try to persuade her she was hallucinating. If she pressed the point, they'd probably sedate her, which would make matters worse. What she needed was time to think.

All of this she'd worked out before they arrived, so that when they asked her what had happened she had her lies ready. It was all a fog, she told them; she could barely remember her own name. It will come back in time, they reassured her, and she replied meekly that she supposed it would. Sleep now, they said, and she told them she'd be happy to do just that, and yawned. They withdrew then.

"Oh, yes . . ." said one of them as he was about to go. "I forgot . . ."

He brought Frank's box from his pocket.

"You were holding on to this," he said, "when you were found. We had the Devil's own job getting it out of your hand. Does it mean anything to you?"

She said it didn't.

"The police have looked at it. There was blood on it, you see. Maybe yours. Maybe not."

He approached the bed.

"Do you want it?" he asked her. Then added, "It has been cleaned."

"Yes," she replied. "Yes, please."

"It may jog your memory," he told her, and put it down on the bedside table.

2

"What are we going to do?" Julia demanded for the hundredth time. The man in the corner said nothing; nor was there any interpretable sign on his ruin of a face. "What did you want with her anyway?" she asked him. "You've spoiled everything."

"Spoiled?" said the monster. "You don't know the meaning of *spoiled.*"

She swallowed her anger. His brooding unnerved her.

"We have to leave, Frank," she said, softening her tone.

He threw a look across at her, white-hot ice.

"They'll come looking," she said. "She'll tell them everything."

"Maybe . . ."

"Don't you *care?*" she demanded.

The bandaged lump shrugged. "Yes," he said. "Of course. But we can't leave, sweetheart." *Sweetheart.* The word mocked them both, a breath of sentiment in a room that had known only pain. "I can't face the world like this." He gestured to his face. "Can I?" he said, staring up at her. "Look at me." She looked. *"Can I?"*

"No."

"No." He went back to perusing the floor. "I need a skin, Julia."

"A skin?"

"Then, maybe . . . maybe we can go dancing together. Isn't that what you want?"

He spoke of both dancing and death with equal nonchalance, as though one carried as little significance as the other. It calmed her, hearing him talk that way.

"How?" she said at last. Meaning, how can a skin be stolen, but also, how will our sanity survive?

"There are ways," said the flayed face, and blew her a kiss.

3

Had it not been for the white walls she might never have picked up the box. Had there been a picture to look at—a vase of sunflowers, or a view of pyramids—anything to break the monotony of the room, she would have been content to stare at it, and think. But the blankness was too much; it gave her no handhold on sanity. So she reached across to the table beside the bed and picked up the box.

It was heavier than she remembered. She had to sit up in bed to examine it. There was little enough to see. No lid that she could find. No keyhole. No hinges. If she turned it over once she turned it half a hundred times, finding no clue to how it might be opened. It was not solid, she was certain of that. So logic demanded that there be a way into it. But where?

She tapped it, shook it, pulled and pressed it, all without result. It was not until she rolled over in bed and examined it in the full glare of the lamp that she discovered some clue as to how the box was constructed. There were infinitesimal cracks in the sides of the box, where one piece of the puzzle abutted the next. They would have been invisible, but that a residue of blood remained in them, tracing the complex relation of the parts.

Systematically, she began to feel her way over the sides, testing her hypothesis by pushing and pulling once more. The cracks offered her a general geography of the toy; without them she might have wandered the six sides forever. But the options were significantly reduced by the clues she'd found; there were only so many ways the box could be made to come apart.

After a time, her patience was rewarded. A click, and suddenly one of the compartments was sliding out from beside its lacquered neighbors. Within, there was beauty. Polished surfaces which scintillated like the finest mother-of-pearl, colored shadows seeming to move in the gloss.

And there was music too; a simple tune emerged from the box, played on a mechanism that she could not yet see. Enchanted, she delved further. Though one piece had been removed, the rest did not come readily. Each segment presented a fresh challenge to fingers and mind, the victories rewarded with a further filigree added to the tune.

She was coaxing the fourth section out by an elaborate series of turns and counter turns, when she heard the bell. She stopped working, and looked up.

Something was wrong. Either her weary eyes were playing tricks or the blizzard-white walls had moved subtly out of true. She put down the box, and slipped out of bed to go to the window. The bell still rang, a solemn tolling. She drew back the curtain a few inches. It was night, and windy. Leaves migrated across the hospital lawn; moths congregated in the lamplight. Unlikely as it seemed, the sound of the bell wasn't coming from outside. It was behind her. She let the curtain drop and turned back into the room.

As she did so, the bulb in the bedside light guttered like a living flame. Instinctively, she reached for the pieces of the box: they and these strange events were intertwined somehow. As her hand found the fragments, the light blew out.

She was not left in darkness however; nor was she alone. There was a soft phosphorescence at the end of the bed, and in its folds, a figure. The condition of its flesh beggared her imagination—the hooks, the scars. Yet its voice, when it spoke, was not that of a creature in pain.

"It's called the Lemarchand Configuration," it said, pointing at the box. She looked down; the pieces were no longer in her hand, but floating inches above her palm. Miraculously, the box was reassembling itself without visible aid, the pieces sliding back together as the whole construction turned over and over. As it did so she caught fresh glimpses of the polished interior, and seemed to see ghosts' faces—twisted as if by grief or bad glass—howling back at her. Then all but one of the segments was sealed up, and the visitor was claiming her attention afresh.

"The box is a means to break the surface of the real," it said. "A kind of invocation by which we Cenobites can be notified—"

"Who?" she said.

"You did it in ignorance," the visitor said. "Am I right?"

"Yes."

"It's happened before," came the reply. "But there's no help for it. No way to seal the Schism, until we take what's ours . . ."

"This is a mistake," she said.

"Don't try to fight. It's quite beyond your control. You have to accompany me."

She shook her head. She'd had enough of bullying nightmares to last her a lifetime.

"I won't go with you," she said. "Damn you, I won't—"

As she spoke, the door opened. A nurse she didn't recognize—a member of the night shift presumably—was standing there.

"Did you call out?" she asked.

Kirsty looked at the Cenobite, then back at the nurse. They stood no more than a yard apart.

"She doesn't see me," it told her. "Nor hear me. I belong to you, Kirsty. And you to me."

"No," she said.

"Are you sure?" said the nurse. "I thought I heard—"

Kirsty shook her head. It was lunacy, all lunacy.

"You should be in bed," the nurse chided. "You'll catch your death."

The Cenobite tittered.

"I'll be back in five minutes," said the nurse. "Please go back to sleep."

And she was gone again.

"We'd better go," it said. "Leave them to their patchwork, eh? Such depressing places."

"You can't do this," she insisted.

It moved toward her nevertheless. A row of tiny bells, depending from the scraggy flesh of its neck, tinkled as it approached. The stink it gave off made her want to heave.

"Wait," she said.

"No tears, please. It's a waste of good suffering."

"The box," she said in desperation. "Don't you want to know where I got the box?"

"Not particularly."

"Frank Cotton," she said. "Does the name mean anything to you? Frank Cotton."

The Cenobite smiled.

"Oh yes. We know Frank."

"He solved the box too, am I right?"

"He wanted pleasure, until we gave it to him. Then he squirmed."

"If I took you to him . . ."

"He's alive then?"

"Very much alive."

"And you're proposing what? That I take him back instead of you?"

"Yes. Yes. Why not? Yes."

The Cenobite moved away from her. The room sighed.

"I'm tempted," it said. Then: "But perhaps you're cheating me. Perhaps this is a lie, to buy you time."

"I know where he *is*, for God's sake," she said. "He did this to me!" She presented her slashed arms for its perusal.

"If you're lying"—it said—"if you're trying to squirm your way out of this—"

"I'm not."

"Deliver him alive to us then . . ."

She wanted to weep with relief.

". . . make him confess himself. And maybe we won't tear your soul apart."

ELEVEN

*R*ory stood in the hallway and stared at Julia, *his* Julia, the woman he had once sworn to have and to hold till death did them part. It had not seemed such a difficult promise to keep at the time. He had idolized her for as long as he could remember, dreaming of her by night and spending the days composing love poems of wild ineptitude to her. But things had changed, and he had learned, as he watched them change, that the greatest torments were often the subtlest. There had been times of late when he would have preferred a death by wild horses to the itch of suspicion that had so degraded his joy.

Now, as he looked at her standing at the bottom of the stairs, it was impossible for him to even remember how good things had once been. All was doubt and dirt.

One thing he was glad of: she looked troubled. Maybe that meant there was a confession in the air, indiscretions that she would pour out and that he would forgive her for in a welter of tears and understanding.

"You look sad," he said.

She hesitated, then said: "It's difficult, Rory."

"What is?"

She seemed to want to give up before she began.

"What is?" he pressed.

"I've so much to tell you."

Her hand, he saw, was grasping the banister so tightly the knuckles burned white. "I'm listening," he said. He would love her again, if she'd just be honest with him. "Tell me," he said.

"I think maybe . . . maybe it would be

easier if I *showed* you . . ." she told him, and so saying, led him upstairs.

<hr />

2

The wind that harried the streets was not warm, to judge by the way the pedestrians drew their collars up and their faces down. But Kirsty didn't feel the chill. Was it her invisible companion who kept the cold from her, cloaking her with that fire the Ancients had conjured to burn sinners in? Either that, or she was too frightened to feel anything.

But then that wasn't how she felt; she *wasn't* frightened. The feeling in her gut was far more ambiguous. She had opened a door—the same door Rory's brother had opened—and now she was walking with demons. And at the end of her travels, she would have her revenge. She would find the thing that had torn her and tormented her, and make him feel the powerlessness that she had suffered. She would watch him squirm. More, she would enjoy it. Pain had made a sadist of her.

As she made her way along Lodovico Street, she looked round for a sign of the Cenobite, but he was nowhere to be seen. Undaunted, she approached the house. She had no plan in mind: there were too many variables to be juggled. For one, would Julia be there? And if so, how involved in all of this was she? Impossible to believe that she could be an innocent bystander, but perhaps she had acted out of terror of Frank; the next few minutes might furnish the answers. She rang the bell, and waited.

The door was answered by Julia. In her hand, a length of white lace.

"Kirsty," she said, apparently unfazed by her appearance. "It's late . . ."

"Where's Rory?" were Kirsty's first words. They hadn't been quite what she'd intended, but they came out unbidden.

"He's here," Julia replied calmly, as if seeking to soothe a manic child. "Is there something wrong?"

"I'd like to see him," Kirsty answered.

"Rory?"

"Yes . . ."

She stepped over the threshold without waiting for an invitation. Julia made no objection, but closed the door behind her.

Only now did Kirsty feel the chill. She stood in the hallway and shivered.

"You look terrible," said Julia plainly.

"I was here this afternoon," she blurted. "I saw what happened, Julia. I *saw.*"

"What was there to see?" came the reply; her poise was unassailed.

"You know."

"Truly I don't."

"I want to speak to Rory . . ."

"Of course," came the reply. "But take care with him, will you? He's not feeling very well."

She led Kirsty through to the dining room. Rory was sitting at the table; there was a glass of spirits at his hand, a bottle beside it. Laid across an adjacent chair was Julia's wedding dress. The sight of it prompted recognition of the lace swath in her hand: it was the bride's veil.

Rory looked much the worse for wear. There was dried blood on his face, and at his hairline. The smile he offered was warm, but fatigued.

"What happened . . . ?" she asked him.

"It's all right now, Kirsty," he said. His voice barely aspired to a whisper. "Julia told me everything . . . and it's all right."

"No," she said, knowing that he couldn't possibly have the whole story.

"You came here this afternoon."

"That's right."

"That was unfortunate."

"You . . . you asked me . . ." She glanced at Julia, who was standing at the door, then back at Rory. "I did what I thought you wanted."

"Yes. I know. I know. I'm only sorry you were dragged into this terrible business."

"You know what your brother's done?" she said. "You know what he summoned?"

"I know enough," Rory replied. "The point is, it's over now."

"What do you mean?"

"Whatever he did to you, I'll make amends—"

"What do you mean, *over*?"

"He's dead, Kirsty."

(". . . *deliver him alive, and maybe we won't tear your soul apart.*")

"Dead?"

"We destroyed him, Julia and I. It wasn't so difficult. He thought he could trust me, you see, thought that blood was thicker than water. Well it isn't. I wouldn't suffer a man like that to live . . ."

She felt something twitch in her belly. Had the Cenobites got their hooks in her already, snagging the carpet of her bowels?

"You've been so kind, Kirsty. Risking so much, coming back here . . ."

(There was something at her shoulder. *"Give me your soul,"* it said.)

"I'll go to the authorities, when I feel a little stronger. Try and find a way to make them understand . . ."

"You killed him?" she said.

"Yes."

"I don't believe it . . ." she muttered.

"Take her upstairs," Rory said to Julia. "Show her."

"Do you want to see?" Julia inquired.

Kirsty nodded and followed.

It was warmer on the landing than below, and the air greasy and gray, like filthy dishwater. The door to Frank's room was ajar. The thing that lay on the bare boards, in a tangle of torn bandaging, still steamed. His neck was clearly broken, head set askew on his shoulders. He was devoid of skin from head to foot.

Kirsty looked away, nauseated.

"Satisfied?" Julia asked.

Kirsty didn't reply, but left the room and stepped onto the landing. At her shoulder, the air was restless.

(*"You lost,"* something said, close by her. *"I know,"* she murmured.)

The bell had begun to ring, tolling for her, surely; and a turmoil of wings nearby, a carnival of carrion birds. She hurried down the stairs, praying that she wouldn't be overtaken before she reached the door. If they tore her heart out, let Rory be spared the sight. Let him remember her strong, with laughter on her lips, not pleas.

Behind her, Julia said, "Where are you going?" When there was no reply forthcoming, she went on talking. "Don't say anything to anybody, Kirsty," she insisted. "We can deal with this, Rory and me—"

Her voice had stirred Rory from his drink. He appeared in the hallway. The wounds Frank had inflicted looked more severe than Kirsty had first thought. His face was bruised in a dozen places, and the skin at his neck plowed up. As she came abreast of him, he reached out and took her arm.

"Julia's right," he said. "Leave it to us to report, will you?"

There were so many things she wanted to tell him at that moment, but time left room for none. The bell was getting louder in her head. Someone had looped their entrails around her neck, and was pulling the knot tight.

"It's too late . . ." she murmured to Rory, and pressed his hand away.

"What do you mean?" he said to her, as she covered the yards to the door. "Don't go, Kirsty. Not yet. Tell me what you mean."

She couldn't help but offer him a backward glance, hoping that he would find in her face all the regrets she felt.

"It's all right," he said sweetly, still hoping to heal her. "Really it is." He opened his arms. *"Come to Daddy,"* he said.

The phrase didn't sound right out of Rory's mouth. Some boys never grew to be daddies, however many children they sired.

Kirsty put out a hand to the wall to steady herself.

It wasn't Rory who was speaking to her. It was Frank. Somehow, it was Frank—

She held on to the thought through the mounting din of bells, so loud now that her skull seemed ready to crack open. Rory was still smiling at her, arms extended. He was talking too, but she could no longer hear what he said. The tender flesh of his face shaped the words, but the bells drowned them out. She was thankful for the fact; it made it easier to defy the evidence of her eyes.

"I know who you are . . ." she said suddenly, not certain of whether her words were audible or not, but unquenchably sure that they were true. Rory's corpse was upstairs, left to lie in Frank's shunned bandaging. The usurped skin was now wed to his brother's body, the marriage sealed with the letting of blood. Yes! That was it.

The coils around her throat were tightening; it could only be moments before they dragged her off. In desperation, she started back along the hallway toward the thing in Rory's face.

"It's you—" she said.

The face smiled at her, undismayed.

She reached out, and snatched at him. Startled, he took a step backward to avoid her touch, moving with graceful sloth, but somehow still managing to avoid her touch. The bells were intolerable; they were pulping her thoughts, tolling her brain tissue to dust. At the rim of her sanity, she reached again for him, and this time he did not quite avoid her. Her nails raked the flesh of his cheek, and the skin, so recently grafted, slid away like silk. The blood-buttered meat beneath came into horrid view.

Behind her, Julia screamed.

And suddenly the bells weren't in Kirsty's

head any longer. They were in the house, in the world.

The hallway lights burned dazzlingly bright, and then—their filaments overloading—went out. There was a short period of total darkness, during which time she heard a whimpering that may or may not have come from her own lips. Then it was as if fireworks were spluttering into life in the walls and floor. The hallway danced. One moment an abattoir (the walls running scarlet); the next, a boudoir (powder blue, canary yellow); the moment following that, a ghost-train tunnel—all speed and sudden fire.

By one flaring light she saw Frank moving toward her, Rory's discarded face hanging from his jaw. She avoided his outstretched arm and ducked through into the front room. The hold on her throat had relaxed, she realized: the Cenobites had apparently seen the error of their ways. Soon they would intervene, surely, and bring an end to this farce of mistaken identities. She would not wait to see Frank claimed as she'd thought of doing; she'd had enough. Instead she'd flee the house by the back door and leave them to it.

Her optimism was short-lived. The fireworks in the hall threw some light ahead of her into the dining room, enough to see that it was already bewitched. There was something moving over the floor, like ash before wind, and chains cavorting in the air. Innocent she might be, but the forces loose here were indifferent to such trivialities; she sensed that to take another step would invite atrocities.

Her hesitation put her back within Frank's reach, but as he snatched at her the fireworks in the hallway faltered, and she slipped away from him under cover of darkness. The respite was all too brief. New lights were already blooming in the hall—and he was after her afresh, blocking her route to the front door.

Why didn't they claim him, for God's sake? Hadn't she brought them here as she'd promised, and unmasked him?

Frank opened his jacket. In his belt was a bloodied knife—doubtless the flaying edge. He pulled it out, and pointed it at Kirsty.

"From now on," he said, as he stalked her, "I'm Rory." She had no choice but to back away from him, the door (escape, sanity) receding with every step. "Understand me? I'm Rory now. And nobody's ever going to know any better."

Her heel hit the bottom of the stair, and suddenly there were other hands on her, reaching through the banisters and seizing fistfuls of her hair. She twisted her head round and looked up. It was Julia, of course, face slack, all passion consumed. She wrenched Kirsty's head back, exposing her throat as Frank's knife gleamed toward it.

At the last moment Kirsty reached up above her head and snatched hold of Julia's arm, wrenching her from her perch on the third or fourth stair. Losing both her balance and her grip on her victim, Julia let out a shout and fell, her body coming between Kirsty and Frank's thrust. The blade was too close to be averted; it entered Julia's side to the hilt. She moaned, then she reeled away down the hall, the knife buried in her.

Frank scarcely seemed to notice. His eyes were on Kirsty once again, and they shone with horrendous appetite. She had nowhere to go but *up*. The fireworks still exploding, the bells still ringing, she started to mount the stairs.

Her tormentor was not coming in immediate pursuit, she saw. Julia's appeals for help had diverted him to where she lay, halfway between stairs and front door. He drew the knife from her side. She cried out in pain, and, as if to assist her, he went down on his haunches beside her body. She raised her arm to him, looking for tenderness. In response, he cupped his hand beneath her head, and drew her up toward him. As their faces came within inches of each other, Julia seemed to realize that Frank's intentions were far from honorable. She opened her mouth to scream, but he sealed her lips with his and began to feed. She kicked and scratched the air. All in vain.

Tearing her eyes from the sight of this depravity, Kirsty crawled up to the head of the stairs.

The second floor offered no real hiding place, of course, nor was there any escape route, except to leap from one of the windows. But having seen the cold comfort Frank had just offered his mistress, jumping was clearly the preferable option. The fall might break every bone in her body, but it would at least deprive the monster of further sustenance.

The fireworks were fizzling out, it seemed; the landing was in smoky darkness. She stumbled along it rather than walked, her fingertips moving along the wall.

Downstairs, she heard Frank on the move again. He was finished with Julia.

Now he spoke as he began up the stairs, the same incestuous invitation:

"Come to Daddy."

It occurred to her that the Cenobites were probably viewing this chase with no little amusement, and would not act until there was only one player left: Frank. She was forfeit to their pleasure.

"Bastards . . ." she breathed, and hoped they heard.

She had almost reached the end of the landing. Ahead lay the junk room. Did it have a window sizable enough for her to climb through? If so, she would jump, and curse them as she fell—curse them all. God and the Devil and whatever lay between, curse them and as she dropped, hope for nothing but that the concrete be quick with her.

Frank was calling her again, and almost at the top of the stairs. She turned the key in the lock, opened the junk room door, and slipped through.

Yes, there was a window. It was uncurtained, and moonlight fell through it in shafts of indecent beauty, illuminating a chaos of furniture and boxes. She made her way through the confusion to the window. It was wedged open an inch or two to air the room. She put her fingers under the frame, and tried to heave it up far enough for her to climb out, but the sash in the window had rotted, and her arms were not the equal of the task.

She quickly hunted for a makeshift lever, a part of her mind coolly calculating the number of steps it would take her pursuer to cover the length of the landing. Less than twenty, she concluded, as she pulled a sheet off one of the tea chests, only to find a dead man staring up at her from the chest, eyes wild. He was broken in a dozen places, arms smashed and bent back upon themselves, legs tucked up to his chin. As she went to cry out, she heard Frank at the door.

"Where are you?" he inquired.

She clamped her hand over her face to stop the cry of revulsion from coming. As she did so, the door handle turned. She ducked out of sight behind a felled armchair, swallowing her scream.

The door opened. She heard Frank's breath, slightly labored, heard the hollow pad of his feet on the boards. Then the sound of the door being pulled to again. It clicked. Silence.

She waited for a count of thirteen, then peeped out of hiding, half expecting him to still be in the room with her, waiting for her to break cover. But no, he'd gone.

Swallowing the breath her cry had been

mounting upon had brought an unwelcome side effect: hiccups. The first of them, so unexpected she had no time to subdue it, sounded gun-crack loud. But there was no returning step from the landing. Frank, it seemed, was already out of earshot. As she returned to the window, skirting the tea-chest coffin, a second hiccup startled her. She silently reprimanded her belly, but in vain. A third and fourth came unbidden while she wrestled once more to lift the window. That too was a fruitless effort; it had no intention of compliance.

Briefly, she contemplated breaking the glass and yelling for help, but rapidly discarded the idea. Frank would be eating out her eyes before the neighbors had even shaken off sleep. Instead she retraced her steps to the door, and opened it a creaking fraction. There was no sign of Frank, so far as her eyes were able to interpret the shadows. Cautiously, she opened the door a little wider, and stepped onto the landing once again.

The gloom was like a living thing; it smothered her with murky kisses. She advanced three paces without incident, then a fourth. On the fifth (her lucky number) her body took a turn for the suicidal. She hiccuped, her hand too tardy to reach her mouth before the din was out.

This time it did not go unheard.

"There you are," said a shadow, and Frank slipped from the bedroom to block her path. He was vaster for his meal—he seemed as wide as the landing—and he stank of meat.

With nothing to lose, she screamed blue murder as he came at her. He was unashamed by her terror. With inches between her flesh and his knife she threw herself sideways and found that the fifth step had brought her abreast of Frank's room. She stumbled through the open door. He was after her in a flash, crowing his delight.

There was a window in this room, she knew; she'd broken it herself, mere hours before. But the darkness was so profound she might have been blindfolded, not even a glimmer of moonlight to feed her sight. Frank was equally lost, it seemed. He called after her in this pitch; the whine of his knife accompanying his call as he slit the air. Back and forth, back and forth. Stepping away from the sound, her foot caught in the tangle of the bandaging on the floor. Next moment she was toppling. It wasn't the boards she fell heavily upon, however, but the greasy bulk of Rory's corpse. It won a howl of horror from her.

"There you are," said Frank. The knife slices were suddenly closer, inches from her head. But she was deaf to them. She had her arms about the body beneath her, and approaching death was nothing beside the pain she felt now, touching him.

"Rory," she moaned, content that his name be on her lips when the cut came.

"That's right," said Frank, "Rory."

Somehow the theft of Rory's name was as unforgivable as stealing his skin; or so her grief told her. A skin was nothing. Pigs had skins; snakes had skins. They were knitted of dead cells, shed and grown and shed again. But a name? That was a spell, which summoned memories. She would not let Frank usurp it.

"Rory's dead," she said. The words stung her, and with the sting, the ghost of a thought—

"Hush, baby . . ." he told her.

—suppose the Cenobites were waiting for Frank to name himself. Hadn't the visitor in the hospital said something about Frank *confessing?*

"You're not Rory . . ." she said.

"*We* know that," came the reply, "but nobody else does . . ."

"Who are you then?"

"Poor baby. Losing your mind, are you? Good thing too . . ."

"Who, though?"

". . . it's safer that way."

"*Who?*"

"Hush, baby," he said. He was stooping to her in the darkness, his face within inches of hers. "Everything's going to be as right as rain . . ."

"Yes?"

"Yes. Frank's here, baby."

"Frank?"

"That's right. I'm *Frank.*"

So saying, he delivered the killing blow, but she heard it coming in the darkness and dodged its benediction. A second later the bell began again, and the bare bulb in the middle of the room flickered into life. By it she saw Frank beside his brother, the knife buried in the dead man's buttock. As he worked it out of the wound he set his eyes on her afresh.

Another chime, and he was up, and would have been at her . . . but for the voice.

It said his name, lightly, as if calling a child out to play.

"Frank."

His face dropped for the second time that night. A look of puzzlement flitted across it, and on its heels, horror.

Slowly, he turned his head round to look at the speaker. It was the Cenobite, its hooks sparkling. Behind it, Kirsty saw three other figures, their anatomies catalogues of disfigurement.

Frank threw a glance back at Kirsty.

"You did this," he said.

She nodded.

"Get out of here," said one of the newcomers. "This isn't your business now."

"Whore!" Frank screeched at her. "Bitch! *Cheating, fucking bitch!*"

The hail of rage followed her across the room to the door. As her palm closed around the door handle, she heard him coming after her, and turned to find that he was standing less than a foot from her, the knife a hair's breadth from her body. But there he was fixed, unable to advance another millimeter.

They had their hooks in him, the flesh of his arms and legs, and curled through the meat of his face. Attached to the hooks, chains, which they held taut. There was a soft sound, as his resistance drew the barbs through his muscle. His mouth was dragged wide, his neck and chest plowed open.

The knife dropped from his fingers. He expelled a last, incoherent curse at her, his body shuddering now as he lost his battle with their claim upon him. Inch by inch he was drawn back toward the middle of the room.

"*Go,*" said the voice of the Cenobite. She could see them no longer; they were already lost behind the blood-flecked air. Accepting their invitation, she opened the door, while behind her Frank began to scream.

As she stepped onto the landing plaster dust cascaded from the ceiling; the house was growling from basement to eaves. She had to go quickly, she knew, before whatever demons were loose here shook the place apart.

But, though time was short, she could not prevent herself from snatching one look at Frank, to be certain that he would come after her no longer.

He was *in extremis,* hooked through in a dozen or more places, fresh wounds gouged in him even as she watched. Spread-eagled beneath the solitary bulb, body hauled to the limits of its endurance and beyond, he gave vent to shrieks that would have won pity from her, had she not learned better.

Suddenly, his cries stopped. There was a pause. And then, in one last act of defiance, he cranked up his heavy head and stared at her, meeting her gaze with eyes from which all bafflement and all malice had fled. They glittered as they rested on her, pearls in offal.

In response, the chains were drawn an inch tighter, but the Cenobites gained no further cry from him. Instead he put his tongue out at Kirsty, and flicked it back and forth across his teeth in a gesture of unrepentant lewdness.

Then he came unsewn.

His limbs separated from his torso, and his head from his shoulders, in a welter of bone shards and heat. She threw the door closed, as something thudded against it from the other side. His head, she guessed.

Then she was staggering downstairs, with wolves howling in the walls, and the bells in turmoil, and everywhere—thickening the air like smoke—the ghosts of wounded birds, sewn wing tip to wing tip, and lost to flight.

She reached the bottom of the stairs, and began along the hallway to the front door, but as she came within spitting distance of freedom she heard somebody call her name.

It was Julia. There was blood on the hall

floor, marking a trail from the spot where Frank had abandoned her, through into the dining room.

"Kirsty . . ." she called again. It was a pitiable sound, and despite the wing-choked air, she could not help but go in pursuit of it, stepping through into the dining room.

The furniture was smoldering charcoal; the ash that she'd glimpsed was a foul-smelling carpet. And there, in the middle of this domestic wasteland, sat a bride.

By some extraordinary act of will, Julia had managed to put her wedding dress on, and secure her veil upon her head. Now she sat in the dirt, the dress besmirched. But she looked radiant nevertheless, more beautiful, indeed, for the fact of the ruin that surrounded her.

"Help me," she said, and only now did Kirsty realize that the voice she heard was not coming from beneath the lush veil, but from the bride's lap.

And now the copious folds of the dress were parting, and there was Julia's head—set on a pillow of scarlet silk and framed with a fall of auburn hair. Bereft of lungs, how could it speak? It spoke nevertheless—

"Kirsty . . ." it said, it begged—and

sighed, and rolled back and forth in the bride's lap as if it hoped to unlodge its reason.

Kirsty might have aided it—might have snatched the head up and dashed out its brains—but that the bride's veil had started to twitch, and was rising now, as if plucked at by invisible fingers. Beneath it, a light flickered and grew brighter, and brighter yet, and with the light, a voice.

"I am the Engineer," it sighed. No more than that.

Then the fluted folds rose higher, and the head beneath gained the brilliance of a minor sun.

She did not wait for the blaze to blind her. Instead she backed out into the hallway—the birds almost solid now, the wolves insane—and flung herself at the front door even as the hallway ceiling began to give way.

The night came to meet her—a clean darkness. She breathed it in greedy gulps as she departed the house at a run. It was her second such departure. God help her, her sanity that there ever be a third.

At the corner of Lodovico Street, she looked back. The house had not capitulated to the forces unleashed within. It stood now as quiet as a grave. No, quieter.

As she turned away somebody collided with her. She yelped with surprise, but the huddled pedestrian was already hurrying away into the anxious murk that preceded morning. As the figure hovered on the outskirts of solidity, it glanced back, and its head flared in the gloom, a cone of white fire. It was the Engineer. She had no time to look away; it was gone again in one instant, leaving its glamour in her eye.

Only then did she realize the purpose of the collision. Lemarchand's box had been passed back to her, and sat in her hand.

Its surfaces had been immaculately resealed, and polished to a high gloss. Though she did not examine it, she was certain there would be no clue to its solution left. The next discoverer would voyage its faces without a chart. And until such time, was she elected its keeper? Apparently so.

She turned it over in her hand. For the frailest of moments she seemed to see ghosts in the lacquer. Julia's face, and that of Frank. She turned it over again, looking to see if Rory was held here: but no. Wherever he was, it wasn't here. There were other puzzles, perhaps, that if solved gave access to the place where he lodged. A crossword maybe, whose solution would lift the latch of the paradise garden, or a jigsaw in the completion of which lay access to Wonderland.

She would wait and watch, as she had always watched and waited, hoping that such a puzzle would one day come to her. But if it failed to show itself she would not grieve too deeply, for fear that the mending of broken hearts be a puzzle neither wit nor time had the skill to solve.

ALSO AVAILABLE BY
CLIVE BARKER

MISTER B. GONE A Novel • ISBN 978-0-06-156249-5 (paperback)
A 600-year-old manuscript, once hidden by Johannes Gutenberg, resurfaces—with a plan to cast the world into darkness and despair.

"Barker confounds expectations once again, giving us one of the most resonant, provocative novels of his career." —*Washington Post*

GALILEE A Novel • ISBN 978-0-06-168427-2 (paperback)
A rich and powerful family's dark, terrible secrets are exposed when an adversarial relationship comes to a head.

"Sexier than King and more inventive than Rice. . . . Full of intense emotions [and] enormous vistas." —*Philadelphia Inquirer*

THE THIEF OF ALWAYS A Novel • ISBN 978-0-06-168426-5 (paperback)
A magical book for readers of all ages, illustrated with more than 40 of Clive Barker's own drawings.

"Barker puts the dark side back into childhood fantasy." —*Publishers Weekly*

THE HELLBOUND HEART A Novel • ISBN 978-0-06-145288-8 (paperback)
Clive Barker's horror masterwork, upon which the cult classic film *Hellraiser* was based.

"The most imaginative of the macabre novelists." —*Kansas City Star*

IMAJICA • **Featuring New Illustrations and an Appendix**
ISBN 978-0-06-093726-3 (paperback)

"Rich in plot twists, byzantine intrigues, and hidden secrets, *Imajica* is a Chinese puzzle box constructed on a universal scale . . . Barker has an unparalleled talent for envisioning other worlds." —*Washington Post Book World*

EVERVILLE • ISBN 978-0-06-093315-9 (paperback)

"Mr. Barker is much more than a genre writer, and his extravagantly unconventional inventions are ingenious refractions of our common quest to experience and understand the mysterious world around us and the mysteries within ourselves."
—*New York Times Book Review*

THE GREAT AND SECRET SHOW • ISBN 978-0-06-093316-6 (paperback)

"A cross between *Gravity's Rainbow* and J.R.R. Tolkein's *Lord of the Rings*, allusive and mythic, complex and entertaining. Extravagantly metaphorical, wildly symbolic." —*New York Times*